风中 SHAOLIN: DANCING IN THE WIND 动少林

齐岸青 著
Written by Qi Anqing

大象出版社
ELEPHANT PRESS

风中 **舞**

SHAOLIN:
DANCING
IN THE WIND

动少林

风中**舞**动少林

SHAOLIN:
DANCING
IN THE WIND

CHAPTER ONE 壹

《风中少林》其实是郑州这座城市的一个梦，

一个在沉重、博大厚土之中追寻轻盈和美丽的梦。

《风中少林》其实也是中原人的寻觅之旅，

一个寻求湮灭已久的浪漫和恣肆的跋涉之旅。

上溯5000年，以土为德的黄帝诞生在这块土地，肇创华夏文明。也许自那时起中原地域演绎的历史剧目，就始终充满深厚、悲壮、磅礴的色彩！沧海桑田，中原人始终首当其冲地承载着时代变迁、王朝更迭的责任和苦难。洛神的惊世姝丽、潘安的悸人颜容早已迷离，列子御风而行的风骨、李商隐泪烛成灰的情痴久已淡然。记忆如同碎片，你要想去连缀它已经困难。只有长久生活在这里的人才能体会，在深厚、恢弘的文化中原寻觅美丽有时会是孤独的跋涉，是对太阳的追赶。

基于对河南历史文化的深思，当时的省委书记李克强和省委宣传部长孔玉芳等构思了"郑汴洛"文艺精品工程，以艺术精品的打造来引领文化事业发展，一幅试图改变河南艺术事业格局的坐标蓝图因此描就。

一个完美的理念需要同样完美而繁杂细致的执行。

在中国优秀艺术作品序列中，大型舞蹈诗《咕哩美》，大型壮族舞剧《妈勒访天边》，南宁国际民歌艺术节……都是璀璨的明珠，它们的光环之后都有一个坚定的身影——南宁和郑州两个城市的前任市委书记李克。李克在文化界远播的声名有时甚至会遮掩他在政界的光彩，对政治和艺术他不仅是一个完美的理想主义者，也同样是一个完美的行为执行者。一个地域文化的漂泊者也许能更深地体味跋涉的孤独，《风中少林》从创意构思、主创选定、剧本修改、剧院构建、演员招聘、导演联排，他都会事必躬亲，谁也无法去究个中原因，只是当《风中少林》横空出世，完美展现之后，我们在幕后看到他眼中的泪花，一下又似乎能触摸到那外婆讲述的遥远故事的缕缕艺术情丝，能倾听到八桂男儿洋溢着中原激情的脉动。

┤ 相 关 链 接 ├

郑州歌舞剧院和《风中少林》

◎2003年12月 舞剧《风中少林》主创人员确定，编剧冯双白，作曲唐建平，舞蹈编导刘晓荷、张弋，武术编导元晖，舞美设计黄楷夫，灯光设计刘建中，服装人物造型设计麦青，艺术总监齐岸青、黄海碧等。剧本开始投入创作。

◎2004年1月13日 郑州歌舞剧院筹备工作领导小组成立，齐岸青任组长，刘宝合任副组长。

◎2004年2月7日 李克书记在京主持《风中少林》剧本（初稿）研讨会。

◎2004年2月8日 演员招聘工作开始。

For the same goal, they join each other in this endeavor. 为了一个共同的目标，他们走到一起

现在的市委书记王文超没有李克这种激情外在,这个骨子里秉承中原文化血脉的前任市长,龙门申报世界遗产,"八大古都"申报和商城遗址改造,嵩山古建筑群申遗……在文化建设文物保护方面他有许多口碑相传的故事,他始终低调地把歌舞剧院和舞剧的构建落在实处,钉在细节。在他身后还有率性睿智的赵建才,温婉历练的杨丽萍……

因为有了这些,一支追赶太阳的队伍出发了……

一支中国最年轻的歌舞剧院团队英姿勃发地开始了自己的旅途。在它蹒跚学步之时,始终有着温暖的手在支撑扶持着它,新任的省委书记徐光春在勾画中原崛起的蓝图时,文化建设文化产业始终是他浓笔重抹的色彩,河南因此有了崭新的外在形象。他留意到了这株新芽,走进排练场、演员宿舍、食堂、舞台,将它的生长放在自己的心胸,《风中少林》团队的每一个节点你都能感到他的关注。他又多次批示并力荐,将舞剧带出河南。

◎ 2004年2月24日 郑州歌舞剧院正式组建,3月16日郑州歌舞剧院挂牌成立,齐岸青兼任院长。

◎ 2004年7月29日 河南省委常委、宣传部长孔玉芳视察歌舞剧院,观看排练。

◎ 2004年10月18日 舞剧《风中少林》在河南人民会堂为首届世界传统武术节作闭幕式演出,受到中外嘉宾一致好评。

◎ 2005年5月9日 《风中少林》提高版首场演出在省人民会堂开演,省委书记徐光春观看了演出并给予高度评价。歌舞剧院股份制改造和体制机制创新的改革计划启动。

◎ 2005年6月24日 《风中少林》在北京保利剧院首场演出,中央政治局常委李长春、文化部部长孙家正、中宣部副部长李丛军在省委书记徐光春、市委书记李克的陪同下观看了演出。

Dancing is intoxicating poetry. 舞蹈就是醉人的诗

　　一个缺失舞蹈的城市突然平添了许多灵动的色彩,风中舞动着少林英雄之幡。

　　走进《风中少林》,你可以聆听到这个团队坚韧的足音,可以从中亲近这片土地,感受其间的那条河、那架山、那段古城、那座庙宇,你会突然发现我们这座城市还有这么多的轻灵和美丽。

这是一个因梦想而充满创造力的团队　　This is a team, full of creativeness to fulfil their dream.

　　◎ 2005年11月7日　河南省委书记徐光春来院调研,郑州中远演艺娱乐有限公司揭牌,宇通集团、建业集团入股。

　　◎ 2005年11月12日　《风中少林》在上海大剧院演出,参加第五届中国荷花奖舞剧比赛演出暨第七届中国上海国际艺术节展演。11月22日,《风中少林》获第五届中国舞蹈荷花奖舞剧评奖作品金奖、导演金奖、服装设计金奖,男主演汪子涵获表演金奖,女主演李倩获表演银奖,群舞演员获集体表演铜奖。

　　◎ 2006年1月6日　《风中少林》入选2005—2006年度国家舞台艺术精品工程初选剧目。

　　◎ 2006年1月12日　《风中少林》获河南省第七届精神文明建设"五个一工程"奖作品特别奖。

① 国家主席胡锦涛在人民大会堂亲切接见剧组演员

The cast were affectionately receieved at the Great Hall of People by Hu Jintao, president of the People's Republic of China.

② 中央政治局常委李长春、文化部部长孙家正、中宣部副部长李丛军在省委书记徐光春、市委书记李克的陪同下观看演出

Mr. Li Changchun, member of the Standing Committee of CPC Central Committee, Mr. Sun Jiazheng, Minister of Culture, and Mr. Li Congjun, Vice-minister of Publicity of the CPC Central Committee, watched the performance with the accompaniment of Mr. Xu Guangchun, secretary of the CPC's Henan Provincial Committee, and Mr. Li Ke, secretary of the CPC's Zhengzhou Municipal Committee.

③ 中央政治局委员，中央书记处书记，中宣部部长刘云山，国务委员陈至立观看演出后接见演员

Mr. Liu Yunshan, member of the Political Bureau of the CPC Central Committee, secretary of the Secretariat of the Central Committee and Head of the Propaganda Department of the CPC Central Committee, and Ms. Chen Zhili, member of the State Council of the People's Republic of China, watched the performance and benignly received the cast.

◎ 2006年2月8—12日 《风中少林》在台北国父纪念馆演出7场，场场爆满，受到热烈欢迎。

◎ 2006年3月10—12日 《风中少林》在北京保利剧院为"两会"代表演出，受到热烈欢迎。中央政治局委员、中央书记处书记、中宣部部长刘云山，国务委员陈至立观看了演出。

◎ 2006年3月30日 《风中少林》为参加丙戌年黄帝故里拜祖大典的嘉宾们作专场演出。全国人大常委会副委员长、民革中央主席何鲁丽，全国政协副主席张思卿等领导和31个国家和地区的世界华人企业家协会的嘉宾观看了演出。

◎ 2006年5月18、19日 《风中少林》为第二届文博会作开幕式演出。

◎ 2006年8月9日 《风中少林》全剧在央视3频道首播。

◎ 2006年8月18日 《风中少林》在北京天桥剧场为外交部驻外使节暨外交部干部职工作专场演出。国务委员唐家璇,外交部长李肇星,外交部党委书记戴秉国等在河南省委书记徐光春,省委常委、常务副省长李克,省委常委、郑州市委书记王文超,郑州市市长赵建才,市委宣传部长杨丽萍等同志的陪同下观看了演出。

◎ 2006年10月18日 《风中少林》在河南省人民会堂接受由文化部艺术司长于平率领的国内文化艺术界著名专家学者、主流媒体记者等一行29人组成的2005—2006年度国家舞台艺术精品工程评审组的验收。

◎ 2006年11月28日 《风中少林》入选2005—2006年度国家舞台艺术精品工程十大精品剧目。

◎ 2007年3月4日 国家主席胡锦涛亲切接见参加元宵节联欢晚会的《风中少林》演员。

◎ 2007年 中宣部将《风中少林》列为全国优秀艺术作品。

追赶太阳…… Chasing the sun...

①②全国人大常委会副委员长、民革中央主席何鲁丽，全国政协副主席张思卿等参加丙戌年黄帝故里拜祖大典，《风中少林》为嘉宾作专场演出
Ms. He Luli, vice chairwoman of the Standing Committee of NPC and chairwoman of Chinese KMT Central Committee, Mr. Zhang Siqing, vice-chairman of CPPCC, and other guests attended the memorial ceremony for the Yellow Emperor in Xinzheng, the native place of the Yellow Emperor, in the Bing-Xu Year. The cast of *Shaolin in the Wind* especially performed for the honored guests.

③国务委员唐家璇、外交部长李肇星观看演出后接见演员
Mr. Tang Jiaxuan, member of the State Council, and Mr. Li Zhaoxing, minister of Foreign Affairs, watched the performance and benignly received the cast.

④河南省委常委、宣传部长孔玉芳视察郑州歌舞剧院，观看排练
Ms. Kong Yufang, member of the Standing Committee of the CPC's Henan Provincial Committee and head of the Publicity Department of the CPC's Henan Provincial Committee, inspected Zhengzhou Song and Dance Theatre and watched the rehearsal.

⑤⑥⑦《风中少林》在台北国父纪念馆演出，受到热烈欢迎
Shaolin in the Wind was performed in Taibei National Dr. Sun Yet-sen Memorial Hall, warmly welcomed and fully attended by the audience.

Shaolin in the Wind (The Saga of a Shaolin Kung-fu Monastic), as a dance drama, is actually a medium supposed to give voice to a fond dream of the populace of Zhengzhou, who have been not only aspiring to gain access to ease and elegance even in their dreams but so overpowered all the time as to remain so far weltering in a sort of mundane vastness.

And this dance drama might as well be visualized as an exploratory and tough pilgrimage embraced by the natives of the Central-China Plains, as pilgrims involved have been bent on reliving the long lost romance and wantonness.

Here is the homeland of the Yellow Emperor, the founder of Sinic culture, whose reign dates way back in the sixth millennium preceding the 1st millennium anno Domini and whose virtue can be epitomized in His Majesty's reverence for Mother Earth. Probably in his era the Central-China Plains was already destined to be the venue for an avalanche of dynastic marches and counter-marches which strike us as most pathetic as well as heroic! Therefore natives of the said plains seemed to have been predestined to take the brunt of all the devastating side of

Related Links

The Annals of Zhengzhou Song and Dance Theatre and *Shaolin in the Wind*

○ In December, 2003, the major working staff of *Shaolin in the Wind* was established and the creating of the scenario began:

Dramaturgy: Feng Shuangbai

Composer: Tang Jianping

Choreographers: Liu Xiaohe, Zhang Yi

Martial Art Choreographer: Yuan Hui

Stage Designer: Huang Kaifu

Lighting Designer: Liu Jianzhong

Costume Designer: Mai Qing

Art Majordomo: Qi Anqing, Huang Haibi, etc.

historical changes in our country.

Many beautiful stories have been widely spread in this beautiful land, including the shocking beauty of the Goddess of the Luo River, the attractive handsomeness of Pan An, the legend about Lie Yukou's riding with the wind and Li Shangyin's loyalty to love. All the stories have gone with the time, and only the fragments of them still remain in people's memory. It's very difficult to stitch them together. Only those who have lived here for a long time can understand that it might be a solitary and hard trudge to seek the beauty of the profound and magnificent culture, just like chasing the sun.

Based on his deep thought on the history and culture of Henan Province, Mr. Li Keqiang, former secretary of the CPC's Henan Provincial Committee, together with Ms. Kong Yufang, head of the Publicity Department of the CPC's Henan Provincial Committee took the leading role in working out the "Zhengzhou-Kaifeng-Luoyang Excellent Works of Literature and Art Project" in order to promote the development of the culture through the creation of excellent works of literature and art. A blueprint to improve the format of the

○ On January 13, 2004, a panel of preparatory work of Zhengzhou Song and Dance Theatre was formed, with Qi Anqing being elected the group leader and Liu Baohe the vice group leader.

○ On February 7, 2004, Secretary of the CPC's Zhengzhou Municipal Committee, Mr. Li Ke hosted the seminar on the scenario of *Shaolin in the Wind* in Beijing.

○ On February 8, 2004, the recruiting of the cast began.

○ On February 24, 2004, Zhengzhou Song and Dance Theatre was formed and the construction began.

○ On March 16, Zhengzhou Song and Dance Theatre hung out its shingle and was formally established. Qi Anqing was elected dean.

○ On July 29, 2004, Ms. Kong Yufang, member of the Standing Committee of the CPC's Henan Provincial Committee and head of the Publicity Department of

汗水从脊背滑落…… Sweat dripping down the back...

the CPC's Henan Provincial Committee, inspected Zhengzhou Song and Dance Theatre and watched the rehearsal.

○ On October 18, 2004, *Shaolin in the Wind* was performed in the closing ceremony of the 1st World Traditional Wushu Festival and was warmly welcomed by the guests from home and abroad.

○ On May 9, 2005, the improved version of *Shaolin in the Wind* was performed in the Great Hall of the People of Henan Province and Mr. Xu Guangchun, secretary of the CPC's Henan Provincial Committee, watched and spoke highly of the dance drama. The shareholding system reform and innovation plan of Zhengzhou Song and Dance Theatre started.

○ On June 24, 2005, *Shaolin in the Wind* was first performed in Beijing Poly Theater. Mr. Li Changchun, member of the Standing Committee of CPC Central

Wishing for soaring in the sky... 希冀飞翔……

Committee, Mr. Sun Jiazheng, minister of Culture, and Mr. Li Congjun, vice-minister of Publicity of the CPC Central Committee, watched the performance with the accompaniment of Mr. Xu Guangchun, secretary of the CPC's Henan Provincial Committee, and Mr. Li Ke, secretary of the CPC's Zhengzhou Municipal Committee.

○ On November 7, 2005, Mr. Xu Guangchun, secretary of the CPC's Henan Provincial Committee, surveyed the work in the theater, and Zhengzhou Zhongyuan Performance and Entertainment Co. Ltd was established, with Yu Tong Group and Jian Ye Group being the shareholders of the company.

○ On November 12, 2005, *Shaolin in the Wind* was performed in Shanghai Grand Theater to take part in the 5th Lotus Award Competition for dance drama and the 7th China Shanghai International Art Festival. On November 22, *Shaolin in the Wind* won the Gold Awards in Dance Drama, Direction, Performance and

culture in Henan Province has thus been made.

A perfect conception needs perfect implementation.

Mr. Li Ke, former secretary of the CPC's Zhengzhou Municipal Committee, a man who came from Guangxi Province, is not only a perfect idealist in art and politics but also a perfect implementer. Having directed the grand song and dance drama "Beautiful Guli", the Zhuang nationality dance drama "Ma'le Visiting the Horizon" and the Nanning International Folk Songs Festival etc., his reputation in the field of culture and art sometimes overshadows his achievements in the political field. As a cultural roamer, he perhaps understands better the loneliness of the long journey to produce a successful dance drama. He was engaged in almost all the work concerning the dance drama *Shaolin in the Wind* such as designing the idea, selecting the producers, revising the scenario, designing and constructing the theater, recruiting the cast, as well as directing and rehearsing the dance drama. Nobody knows why he takes care of everything himself. Only when the dance drama was performed perfectly on the stage, and when we saw him backstage, tears in his eyes, did we understand

Costume Design in the 5th Lotus Award Competition. The leading actor Wang Zihan won the Gold Award of Performance, the leading actress the Silver Award of Performance, and the other dancers the Bronze Award of Performance.

○ On January 6, 2006, *Shaolin in the Wind* was nominated for the preliminary list of "National Fine Stage Works of Art Project 2005-06".

○ On January 12, 2006, *Shaolin in the Wind* won the Special Production Award of the 7th Spiritual Civilization Construction——"Five Ones Project" in Henan Province.

○ On February 8-12, 2006, *Shaolin in the Wind* was performed successively in Taibei National Dr. Sun Yet-sen Memorial Hall for seven times, warmly welcomed and fully attended by the audience.

○ On March 10-12, 2006, *Shaolin in the Wind* was performed in Beijing Poly

that it is simply because of his love for the Chinese art and culture, and his love for the Central-China Plains.

Without the similar outward passion that Li Ke has, Mr. Wang Wenchao, the present secretary of the CPC's Zhengzhou Municipal Committee, and a native of the Central-China Plains, has unusually ardent love for this vast land and can very well match Li Ke in unparalleled devotion to Zhengzhou. As the former mayor of the city of Zhengzhou, he is innately well related to the splendid culture here. He has contributed much to the protection and development of the Central-China Plains' culture, the Dragon Gate Grottoes' application for the World Legacy, Zhengzhou's application for "Eight Ancient Capitals" of China, the reconstruction of the ruins of the capital of the Shang Dynasty, and the application of the ancient building complex in Mt. Song for the World Legacy. Without attracting much public attention, he has done a lot for *Shaolin in the Wind*, such as the creation of the dance drama and the construction of the theater. Much work has been jointly done by the wise and open-minded Zhao Jiancai and the gentle and capable Yang Liping.

Theater for the representatives of the two national conferences of CPC and CPPCC and was warmly welcomed. Mr. Liu Yunshan, member of the Political Bureau of the CPC Central Committee, secretary of the Secretariat of the Central Committee and head of the Propaganda Department of the CPC Central Committee, and Ms. Chen Zhili, member of the State Council of the People's Republic of China, watched the performance.

○ On March 30, 2006, *Shaolin in the Wind* was especially performed in the Bing-Xu Year (or the Year of Dog according to the Chinese lunar calendar) for the honored guests attending the memorial ceremony for the Yellow Emperor, the well-known legendary ancestor of Chinese people, in Xinzheng, the native place of the Yellow Emperor. Ms. He Luli, vice chairwoman of the Standing Committee of NPC and chairwoman of Chinese KMT Central Committee, Mr. Zhang Siqing, vice-

Thanks to them, a team chasing the sun sets out ...

Then, the youngest song and dance theatre in China commences its journey. In the very beginning, it gets the support from the newly-appointed secretary of the CPC's Henan Provincial Committee, Mr. Xu Guangchun. In his blueprint of developing the Central-China Plains, cultural construction is one of the important tasks for him. Therefore, he has always kept an eye on the dance drama *Shaolin in the Wind*, discussing it with the cast and the major working members in the rehearsal place, in their dormitories, in the

无论是白天…… Rehearsals in the daytime...

chairman of CPPCC, and other guests who were the members of World Chinese Entrepreneur Association from about 31 countries and regions watched the performance.

○ On May 18 and 19, 2006, *Shaolin in the Wind* was performed in the opening ceremony of the 2nd China International Cultural Industry Fair.

○ On August 9, 2006, *Shaolin in the Wind* was first broadcast by CCTV-3.

○ On August 18, 2006, *Shaolin in the Wind* was especially performed in Beijing Tianqiao Theater for the staff of the ministry of foreign affairs. Member of the State Council, Mr. Tang Jiaxuan, minister of foreign affairs, Mr. Li Zhaoxing, and secretary of the Ministry of Foreign Affairs, Mr. Dai Bingguo, accompanied by the chief leaders of Henan Province, Mr. Xu Guangchun, Mr. Li Ke, Mr. Wang Wenchao, Mr. Zhao Jiancai and Ms. Yang Liping, watched the performance.

dining room, and on the stage, caring about every stage of the dance drama.

While you are watching the dance drama *Shaolin in the Wind*, you will get to know how talented and enthusiastic the creation team is, you will experience how beautiful and old the river, the mountain and the temple are, and you will find how energetic and brisk our city is.

Rehearsals in the evenings...　还是黑夜······

○ On October 18, 2006, *Shaolin in the Wind* was performed in the Great Hall of the People in Henan Province to be checked and accepted by the appraising panel for the "National Fine Stage Works of Art Project 2005-06". The panel consisted of 29 members, including famous experts in the field of culture and art, and reporters of mainstream mass media, which was headed by Mr. Yu Ping, director of Art Department of the Ministry of Culture.

○ On November 28, 2006, *Shaolin in the Wind* was chosen to be the top 10 fine stage works of art of the "National Fine Stage Works of Art Project 2005-06".

○ On March 4, 2007, Hu Jintao, President of the People's Republic of China, affecionately receieved the cast of *Shaolin in the Wind*, who participated in the Lantern Festival Gala.

风中 SHAOLIN: DANCING IN THE WIND 动少林

CHAPTER TWO 贰

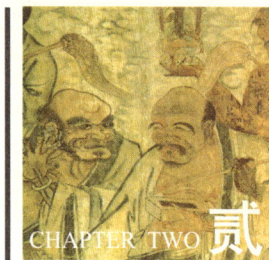

　　黄河是被一个民族誉为母亲的河。她的身躯像舒缓躺卧的母亲绵延千里不绝，河的源头是母亲神秘而高扬的头颅，那云雾缭绕、白雪皑皑的高原如同她美丽、洁净的容颜，冰冷、清澈的细流蜿蜒如云黛青发，慢慢汇拢来生命之水。大

郑州黄河国家地质公园　Zhengzhou Yellow River National Geopark

河经历过千里跌宕，清澈，浑浊，流淌到中原变得温厚，柔润，奔涌成宽广和包容，成为河流的腹脐之处。这里是最神秘、最撩人心魄的地方，河流的魂是由这生命之壶而孕育的，生命最初的孕育和裂变，都是由这辉煌与苦难混沌的生命之涡沁入子孙血液。河流两侧肥沃的土地是她的分娩。这里我们也可以把她看成母亲凹凸有致、丰韵多姿的背部，风情万千，旖旎妖娆，低吟浅唱无数浪漫乐章。河流的笑靥春情，如乳浆般让人嗅之即醉。再去婉转下泻，该是母亲修长丰盈的双腿，静静躺在平原之间，流水偶尔在膝部有些跌宕，沿着拱成弯月的素足逶迤汇入蓝色的海洋。

嵩山峭岩 Lofty and Steep Mount Song

嵩山是一座"峻极于天"的山，是中华民族的父亲山，他用11亿年的时间在海水与岩浆中默然地铸造自己的骨骼，镌刻自己的容颜。25亿年前跃出海面时他已是屹立群山中的一位睿智的长者，他用深邃的目光俯瞰人世，用自己风骨料峭的身躯最早见证了沧海桑田的故事。他又是充满激情活力的青年，亿万年来始终躁动着，不安分地构造着自己的身体。他是给这块柔润、温软土壤以铁骨精血的男人。在中原，嵩山是汪洋

相 关 链 接

黄河

华夏文明发祥之水，我国第二条大河。源出青海省巴颜喀拉山脉雅拉达泽山东麓的约古宗列盆地，流经青海、四川、甘肃、宁夏、内蒙古、陕西、山西、河南、山东9个省区，在山东垦利县境入海。干流全长5464公里，流域面积75.24万平方公里。

郑州桃花峪为黄河中游与下游的分界点。

恣肆的另类，张扬，叛逆，充满英雄激情，吸引了无数的帝
王将相、高僧名道、文人骚客在这里游幸封禅、授徒传教，
在亿年峭壁上留下厚重的文化肌理。

Statues of the Fire Emperor and the Yellow Emperor　炎黄二帝塑像

黄帝

中华民族的共同祖先，姓
公孙，名轩辕，号有熊。生于轩
辕之丘（今郑州新郑市），故称
轩辕氏。继其父少典为有熊部
落首领，代神农氏而有天下，都
于有熊（今郑州新郑市），世称
黄帝。蚕桑、舟、车、文字、音
律、算术均创始于黄帝时代。

The Native Place of the Yellow Emperor in Xinzheng　新郑黄帝故里

嵩山　Mount Song

郑州之城是中国城市文明史第一座都城,汤伐夏都亳,在这里建立商王朝,开启了郑州,也开创了中国都市历史。

在中国八大古都北京、西安、洛阳、南京、开封、杭州、安阳、郑州之中,郑州是近两年才写进这个序列的,很多人对此还不太熟悉。郑州辉煌的都市历史离我们过于遥远,文字、口传的故事和记忆如同彩陶,虽也斑斓但已成碎片。即使河南的四大古都之中,郑州也缺少汉唐洛阳的辉煌浪漫,大宋汴梁的繁华绮丽,晚商安阳的甲骨遗韵。可因为有了"郑州商城",这一切又有了别样的书写方式,郑州毋庸置疑地跻身中国古都和世界历史都市之列。

1950年秋天,一位叫韩维周的小学教师在郑州二里岗一带不经意地发现了一些绳纹陶片和磨制石器,引起国家和省市文物专家的注意,他们沿着最初误认为的"隆起土岗"或"废遗河堤"寻觅,却不断发现商代器物和夯土层,于是,一个世界上现存最早、最完整的郑州商代遗址拂去了历史厚土,呈现在世人面前。

洛神

洛水之神名曰宓妃,相传为伏羲的女儿,寓居之处为今郑州巩义伊洛河汇流地。后溺于洛水,被天帝封为洛神。另有传说宓妃是洛河美丽动人的渔家女儿,洛河水伯经常兴风作浪,闹得洛河沿岸民不聊生。河伯声言,只要宓妃嫁给他,便不再作恶。宓妃为救百姓,与父母乡亲洒泪分别,从容走入河内。从此洛河风浪平息,百姓安居乐业。人们为了纪念宓妃,为她兴庙宇塑金身,尊她为"洛河娘娘",至今在巩义市回郭镇刘村每年农历六月二十三日的庙会上,四村八乡的民众还会汇聚于此,举行隆重的祭祀大典。

经过50余年的考古发掘，证实郑州商城是一个总面积约25平方公里，由宫城、内城、外城所组成的古代都市。其内城城垣周长达7公里。宫城内分布有数十处大型夯土基址，宫殿区内还有祭祀遗址。外城内发现2处铸铜作坊、1处制陶作坊和1处制骨作坊遗址，还有4处墓葬区。郑州商城完备的城郭制将中国城市城郭建制史提前了数百年。可以说郑州商城是迄今为止考古发掘的最早的建制最为完善的城市。

Ruins of the Capital of the Shang Dynasty in Zhengzhou　郑州商城遗址

Painting of *Ode to the Goddess of the Luo River*　洛神赋图

郑州商城的年代，经过碳14测定，最早为公元前1600年，最晚为公元前1415年。该城作为都城共沿用了215年，它的建城时间最少达3600年。郑州商城的性质，由最早的商城隞都说，到隞都与亳都二说并行，直到亳都说形成基本定论，夏商周断代工程专家组认定"郑州商城和偃师商城基本同时或略有先后,是商代最早的两处具有都邑规模的遗址,推断其分别为汤所居之亳和汤灭夏后在下洛之阳所建之'宫邑'亦即'西亳'……"商汤开国以后，太丁、外丙、中壬、太甲、沃丁、太庚、小甲、雍己、太戊

郑州商城遗址出土的青铜器 Bronze Ware Unearthed in the Ruins of the Capital of the Shang Dynasty in Zhengzhou
郑州商城上战国时代的铲痕 Marks of Shovels Left from the Warring States Period on the City Walls of the Capital of the Shang Dynasty in Zhengzhou

潘安

潘安（247—300年），又名潘岳，字安仁，郑州中牟人，西晋文学家。他善诗赋，诗文词藻艳丽，尤工哀诔，与潘勖、潘尼被文坛并称为"三潘"，在文学史上有较高地位。

潘安风姿秀美，容貌出众，《晋书·潘

Tomb of Pan An 潘安墓

共9王沿用了汤都，其积年与考古发现的郑州商城的积年相吻合，因此郑州商城为亳都，已成定论。

原国家文物局局长张文彬先生说："郑州为汤都亳的历史地位已是无可辩驳的事实。……郑州商城其规模之大，都城规划布局之严整，内涵之丰富，气魄之宏伟，堪称当时世界之最。它不仅是公元前1600年中国政治、经济、文化的中心，也是同时代的世界文明中心之一。"与郑州商城同时期的世界其他文明，如两河流域的巴比伦城（前1894—前1595年）、亚达城（前1500年左右）、印度河流域的摩亨佐·达罗城和哈巴拉城，还有尼罗河流域的埃及十七王朝和十八王朝早期的一些城市相比，即使它们最兴盛时，规模和建制都比不上郑州商城。郑州商城不仅在郑州的发展史上有着里程碑的意义，它在中国古代乃至世界历史上，也是一座著名的早期都城。

Ruins of the Capital of the Shang Dynasty in Zhengzhou　郑州商城遗址

岳传》载："岳美姿仪，辞藻绝丽。……少时常挟弹出洛阳道，妇人遇之者，皆连手萦绕，投之以果，遂满车而归。"

New Year Picture of "Throwing Fruits at Pan An"　年画《潘安掷果》

郑州地区还存在一个古都城群,如黄帝的西山古城,祝融氏的新密古城寨,夏禹的登封阳城,夏启的新密新寨古城,商中丁的小双桥隞都遗址,春秋战国时代的郑韩故城等。走在今日郑州的中心城区和周边辖区,你能很容易踏上那黄土叠压起的厚厚的城垣,纵情想象帝王公侯之都的繁华情景,可许多的老郑州不在意这些,他们只是已习惯于在土墙上散步,邻里之间的琐屑杂事和古墙的宏大诉说已经融为他们日常的生活。

登封阳城遗址　Ruins of Yangcheng City at Dengfeng

列子

列御寇(前450?—前375年?),一作圄寇、围寇,史称列子,郑国圃田(今郑州)人。终生致力于道德学问,不求名利。隐居四十年,潜心学问,尊崇黄老,主张循名责实、无为而治。现有《列子》八篇。唐代被尊奉为四大真人之一,其书《列子》被尊为《冲虚真经》。"其学本于黄帝、老子,号曰道家。"

列子像　Picture of Lie Zi

　　虽然历史的背影远逝,但那不曾消失的残垣和泥土宛如记忆的碎片,依然能够描述这里3600年前曾有的骄傲,倾听绵延千年历史的足音,楚汉鸿沟之金戈铁马厮杀之声,溱洧青水绿春中悠悠郑风靡靡卫音,汉墓唐窟砖雕石刻上弄影起舞的衣袖窸窣……

Cite of the Old Stockaded Village at Xinmi　新密古城寨城址

郑州列子墓
Tomb of Lie Zi in Zhengzhou

郑州列子祠
The Ancestral Temple of Lie Zi in Zhengzhou

少林寺　Shaolin Buddhist Monastery

　　少林寺是禅宗祖庭，有"天下第一名刹"之称，达摩面壁的造影已是千年遗痕，慧可立雪自悟的坚忍成为中原的余韵。少林寺其实又是一种符号，是江湖侠骨、武林义风的象征，千百年来它造就了无数英雄梦想。至今这里的暮鼓晨钟、高塔飞檐，仍是现代都市的一抹绚丽曙色……

　　是《风中少林》，让我们透过慈悲为怀、危难济世的英雄故事，透过威风八面、气吞山河的少林功夫，重新感受这座城市的河流、山脉、城垣、寺院……拂去风尘遮掩放飞梦想，抹开云烟湮泯澄清美丽。当少林在风中舞动的时候，舞动的其实是一座城市——一座城市的个性、一座城市的气质、一座城市的涵养、一座城市的灵魂。

The Yellow River has long been regarded as the mother river of the Chinese nation. Winding endlessly for thousands of *li*, it is like a mother lying with relaxation and elegance. The headstream of the river is like her mysterious and high-rising head, the cloudy and snow-covered plateau being her beautiful and neat forehead, and the icy and clear trickling flows being her black hair, and all these have gradually combined to form one stream of life. After thousands of *li*'s turbulent running, the Yellow River becomes very wide and gentle in central China. The stretch of the Yellow River in central China is like her main body, the most mysterious and spellbound place, a place of breeding new life. Its water is like the milk of a mother, and rich fields on both sides of the river are her children. We can also take this stretch of the river as the back of a mother, being graceful, plump and romantic. Then come the mother's legs, flowing quietly though the plains, occasionally raging violently, and slowly merging into the blue sea.

Mt. Song is a hill which has been claimed "higher than the sky" and is regarded as the father mountain of the Chinese nation. He spent 1.1 billion years in casting his ribs

Related Links
The Yellow River

The Yellow River, the birthplace of Chinese civilization, is the second longest river in China. It originates from Yueguzonglie Basin, east of Mount Yagradagzê of the majestic Bayankera Mountains in Qinghai Province, traversing through nine provinces of Qinghai Province, Sichuan Province, Gansu Province, Ningxia Hui Nationality Autonomous Region, Inner Mongolia, Shaanxi Province, Shanxi Province, Henan Province and Shandong Province before merging into the sea in Kenli county of Shandong Province and flowing into the Bohai Sea. The length of the main stream reaches 5,464 kilometres and its drainage area covers 752,400 square kilometres.

Taohuayu (meaning "Valley of Peach Blossom") of Zhengzhou is the dividing-line of the middle reach and the lower reach of the Yellow River. Its middle

and carving his features silently in sea waters and magma. Two and a half billion years ago, when he leapt out of the sea level, he had been a wise old man standing among the mountains. Since then, he has been looking out upon the world with his keen eyes and witnessing the life of people with his body. He has also been an energetic and enthusiastic young man, always structuring his body restlessly, infusing his spirit into the gentle and soft land. As a hero full of treasonous and passionate spirit, Mt. Song has attracted numerous kings and generals in ancient times to hold ceremonies to worship gods in the heaven, numerous eminent monks and famous Taoist priests to propagate doctrines to their disciples, and many men of letters to inscribe their poems and essays on the billion-year-old rocks.

Zhengzhou (Bo in ancient China) was chosen to be the capital of the Shang Dynasty after King Tang defeated the king of the Xia Dynasty, thus starting the civilization history of Chinese city.

The recent two years saw Zhengzhou being listed among the Eight Ancient Capitals of China (including Beijing, Xi'an, Luoyang, Nanjing, Kaifeng, Hangzhou, and Anyang),

reaches end at Taohuayu in Zhengzhou City, Henan Province. Here the Yellow River splits the Loess Plateau in half, forming the longest continuous gorge in the whole drainage area of the river. The Yellow River's lower reaches end in a delta on the Bohai Sea.

Huayuankou of the Yellow River 黄河花园口

although many people are not familiar with this fact. The
reason is that its brilliant history as a capital is so remote
that people have ignored it for a long time though there
are some written records and stories spread from mouth
to mouth. Even among the four ancient capitals in Henan
Province, Zhengzhou lacks the brilliance and romance of
Luoyang as the capital of the Han Dynasty and the Tang
Dynasty, the prosperity of business in Kaifeng as the capital of the Northern Song Dynasty, and the cultural appeal
of the inscriptions on bones or tortoise shells in Anyang
as the capital of the late period of the Shang Dynasty. But
the situation has changed since the discovery of
Zhengzhou being the capital of the Shang Dynasty.
Zhengzhou ranks undoubtedly among the ancient capitals of China as well as the ancient cities of historical im-
portance in the world.

In autumn of 1950, a primary school teacher named
Han Weizhou found some thread-grained pottery pieces and
grinded stoneware in Erligang of Zhengzhou without any
intention. This attracted some archaeologists' attention.
They went to investigate the places which had been mis-

The Yellow Emperor

The Yellow Emperor, a
legendary king and ancestor of
the Chinese nation, whose sur-
name is Gong Sun, given name
Xuan Yuan, assumed name
You Xiong, was born on a hilly
terrain at Xuanyuan (now in
Xinzheng of Zhengzhou, Henan
Province). Therefore he also
went by the name of Xuan Yuan. Having inherited his monarchy from his father, he
became the leader of the Youxiong tribe and, after having defeated Shen Nong

黄帝故里黄帝塑像　Statue of the Yellow Emperor in the Native Place of the Yellow Emperor

taken as "the risen heap" and "the discarded river bank", and they discovered some historical relics of the Shang Dynasty and rammed-earth architectural foundation successively. Thus the site of the ancient capital of the Shang Dynasty in Zhengzhou, which proves to be the earliest and the best preserved one in the world, was discovered.

After 50 years of excavation and archaeological studies, Zhengzhou, which is made of the palace city, the inner city and the outer city with a perimeter of seven kilometers, and covers an area of 25 square kilometers, has been proved to be the ancient capital of the Shang Dynasty. Distributed in the palace city are over ten sites of earth compaction, and sites for sacrifice are found in the palace city. Inside the city, people have found four workshops, two for making bronze ware, one for pottery, one for bone objects, and four sections of tombs. The complete urban system of Zhengzhou as the capital of the Shang Dynasty brings the history of urban system in China forward for hundreds of years to an earlier period in history. It can be regarded as the earliest established ancient city unearthed up to now.

(also called the Fire Emperor, a legendary king of ancient China), was enthroned as a sovereign of the whole country. He decided on Youxiong (now Xinzheng city of Zhengzhou) as the capital. The later generation of Chinese people has addressed him as the Yellow Emperor in history. The handicraft of planting mulberries and raising silkworms, the making of boats and carts, the development of written language, music and arithmetic all started from the time of the Yellow Emperor.

Tested with C14 dating for dynastic history used in archeological research, the history of Zhengzhou as the ancient capital of the Shang Dynasty can be traced to a period as early as 1600 B.C. or as late as 1415 B.C., existing as a capital for about 215 years, that is to say, it has a history of at least 3,600 years.

There are a variety of arguments about the history of Zhengzhou as the capital of the Shang Dynasty. Among them the argument which states that the ancient capital was built at Ao, is the earliest one. It is followed by another argument which emphasizes the simultaneous existence of both Ao and Bo as the capital. The finally decided argument is that Bo was the capital. Experts researching the dynastic history of the Xia, the Shang and the Zhou Dynasties held that Zhengzhou and Yanshi were possibly the capital city of the Shang Dynasty at the same period or successively in time and they were both the relics of the earliest places with the size of a city or state. They made a conclusion that Zhengzhou and Yanshi were respectively the site of Bo occupied by King Tang of the Shang Dynasty, and the site of West Bo, established in Luoyang after King Tang overthrew

Goddess of the Luo River

Goddess of the Luo River, also called Fufei, is said to be the daughter of Fu Xi (also called the Blue Emperor, the earliest ancestor of the Chinese nation who taught the use of the net in fishing. He is said to have developed the Chinese method of writing, which are drawn like little nets), living in the place where the Luo River and the Yi River (two tributaries of the Yellow River) converge in Gongyi of Zhengzhou. She was drowned in the Luo River and was entitled the Goddess of the Luo River by the Jade-Emperor (Supreme God of Chinese folk religion, supreme Heavenly Ruler, and Emperor of the Universe). Another legend says that she is a daughter of a fisherman, beautiful and hard-working. At that time, a monster in the Luo River frequently jumps out of the river to bring disasters to the people living along the river. The people there live a miserable life. The monster

the Xia Dynasty. After King Tang commenced the Shang Dynasty, nine kings after him kept this capital, including King Taiding, King Waibing, King Zhongren, King Taijia, King Woding, King Taigeng, King Xiaojia, King Yongji and King Taiwu. The total length of time during their reigns accorded with the existing period of Zhengzhou as the capital of the Shang Dynasty. Therefore, the argument has been settled that Zhengzhou is the right site for Bo as the capital of Shang Dynasty.

The former Director of State Historic Relics Bureau, Mr. Zhang Wenbin says: "It is undeniable that Zhengzhou is Bo, the ancient capital of the Shang Dynasty. It can be regarded as the best capital of the world at that time, for its size is so big, its planning so standardized, its essence so profound and its spirit so magnificent...As proved in written record, it was not only the political, economic and cultural center of China in the year of 1600 B.C., but also one of the centers of contemporaneous civilizations in the world." Other contemporaneous civilizations include the city of Babylon in the Euphrates and Tigris valley existing between 1894 B.C. and 1595 B.C., the city of Ada existing in about

declares that if Fufei marries him, he would not attack people any more. In order to protect the people there, Fufei accepts the request of the monster. After saying goodbye to her parents and neighbors, she throws herself into the river and marries the monster. After that, the monster does not appear any more, and peace returns to people's life again. To commemorate this beautiful girl forever, people build a temple and make a statue for her in Liu village, Huiguo Town, Gongyi City, addressing her respectfully as the Empress of the Luo River. Since then, on June 23 of the Chinese lunar calendar every year, there has been a temple fair for people to pay tribute to her. People in this area gather here to hold a grand ceremony and offer sacrifice to her.

1500 B.C., the cities of Mohenjo-Dara and Harappa in the Indus valley and other cities in the Nile valley in the 17th and early 18th dynasties in ancient Egypt, etc. Compared with them, even in the most prosperous period of these cities, Zhengzhou, as the capital of the Shang Dynasty, was unexampled in the aspect of size and structure. Zhengzhou as the capital of the Shang Dynasty is a milestone in its history of development. It is regarded as a famous capital city in Chinese history as well as in the world history.

There are also a group of ancient cities in this region, including the Old City built by the Yellow Emperor at West Hill, the old stockaded village built by the Zhu Rong family (descendants of the Yellow Emperor) at Xinmi, the Yangcheng city built by King Yu of the Xia Dynasty in Dengfeng, the old city built by King Qi of the Xia Dynasty at Xinzhai in Xinmi, the relics of Ao as the capital of the Shang Dynasty built by King Zhongding at Xiaoshuangqiao, the old cities of the states of Zheng and Han during the Spring and Autumn Period (770 B.C.-476 B.C.). Walking in the downtown and the surrounding areas of Zhengzhou today, you are likely walking on the thick walls covered by dust and

Pan An

Pan An (247-300), the well-known handsome man in Chinese history, was born in Zhongmu of Zhengzhou. Another name of his is Pan Yue, his given name An Ren, a man of letters of the Western Jin Dynasty. Being good at writing poems, fugues and *ailei* (which is equal to elegies in English), he is often addressed together with Pan Xu and Pan Ni as the "Three Pans" in the literary circles, and has occupied an important place in the history of literature.

It is recorded in the book *History of Jin·Biography of Pan Yue* that Pan An was very handsome and elegant. It says: "Pan Yue is very handsome and his poems are beautiful and magnificent... When he was young, whenever he went out of Luoyang city with his catapult to hunt, women who met him would walk around his cart, hand in hand, and throw many fruits into his cart until it was full. Then he would return with a cart full of fruits."

can't help imagining the hustle and bustle in the city ever inhabited by emperors and their officials in ancient China. Many residents who have lived here for many years have become accustomed to walking on the earthen walls without taking much notice of its splendid past. The trivialities in the neighborhood and the anecdotes about the age-old walls have melted into their daily life.

Though all this has passed away, from the never-vanishing ruins and earth, we can still describe its pride and prosperity which existed 3,600 years ago, we can still hear the footsteps of the history, the shouting and crying of soldiers and tingling of shining spears and armored horses in the ancient battle between the state of Chu and the state of Han, the pleasant music in the style of *Ode of Zheng* around the Zhen River and the Wei River, the rustling sound of the sleeves of dancers carved in rocks and bricks in the graves of the Han Dynasty and the grottoes of the Tang Dynasty...

In Shaolin Buddhist Monastery, the "unparalleled Buddhist monastic institution under heaven" and "the Buddhist Ch'an sect's Ancestral Court", we can still feel the shadow

Lie Zi

Lie Zi ("zi" means "master" or "teacher") (450 B.C.?-375 B.C.?) was born in Putian in the State of Zheng(now Zhengzhou city). His full name was Lie Yukou (Lieh Yu-khau in English). Devoted all his life to improve his own learning and cultivation instead of pursuing fame and interest, he lived in seclusion for about forty years. He admired the Yellow Emperor and Lao Zi (the founder of Taoism in China) and advocated tacit governing with non-doing. There are eight articles in his works *Lie-zi*. He was addressed respectfully as one of the four great True Men, and his works *Lie-zi* was considered to be a major text in the Taoist canon and was confirmed in 742 when the Tang emperor Hsuan-tsung bestowed upon the text the title *Chong Xu Zhen Jing (The True Classic of Vacuity)*. In 1007 the Sung emperor Chen-zong enlarged the title to *Ch'ung-hsu chih-te chen-ching (The True Classic*

of Bodhidharma facing the wall, a story spread for thousands of years, and can still be excited by the firmness and persistence of Hui-Ke who stood in snow till it covered his knees waiting for Bodhidharma's acceptance of him to be his disciple. In fact, Shaolin Buddhist Monastery is also a symbol of knighthood and chivalry of traditional Chinese martial artists. Furthermore, Shaolin Buddhist Monastery has also made numerous people's dream of becoming heroes come true. Still, the sound of ringing a bell in the early morning and beating a drum in the evening, and the scenery of ancient high towers and pavilions with eaves are an important part of the modern city.

It is the heroic stories and the conquering and awe-inspiring Shaolin Kung Fu in *Shaolin in the Wind* that make us know the river, the mountain, the city and the monastery better, to let our dreams go freely which have been covered with dust, and to enjoy the beauty which has long been overshadowed with smoke. Actually, what the dance drama tries to display is the essence of our city, its verve, its temperament, its self-restraint and its soul.

of Supreme Virtue and Vacuity). Learning from the Yellow Emperor and Lao-tzu, he is regarded as a Taoist scholar.

Notes: The Indus Valley civilization grew up along the banks of the Indus River in what is now Pakistan. The two most important sites uncovered so far by archeologists are Harappa and Mohenjo-Dara; both cities show considerable development including multi-level houses and city-wide plumbing.

Cultural Relic of the Shang Dynasty Unearthed in the Capital of the Shang Dynasty in Zhengzhou　郑州商城出土的商代文物

风中
SHAOLIN:
DANCING
IN THE WIND
动少林

CHAPTER THREE 叁

　　巨幅的纱幕垂落舞台前沿,纱幕上的岩壁和舞台后的山岩呼应,若隐若现,超然峻拔之中透出丝丝神秘。

　　在《风中少林》气势如虹、异彩纷呈的舞台上,移动的塔林、倾斜的牌坊、倒伏的石狮都传递着一种力度,一种内涵,让人在身临其境中有驰骋忘归的生命体验。而最给人以心灵震撼的,无疑是舞台深处那面厚重的岩壁石崖。它其实就是嵩山三皇寨普通峭岩的拷贝,舞台上它是唯一未经粉饰

相 关 链 接

嵩山峭岩

　　嵩山地层构造有重要的地学对比意义。其珍贵地质遗迹是研究地壳演化规律、追溯地球演化历史的完美地域。嵩山地区连续完整地袒露着太古宙、元古宙、古生代、中生代、新生代五个地质时期的沉积和构造的序列产物,清晰地保存着发生在25亿年前的嵩阳运动、18亿年前的中岳运动、5.43亿年前的少林运动三次全球性前寒武纪造山、造陆运动所形成的不整合接触界面及构造形态遗迹。尤其是少室山三皇寨直立的石英岩层与尖棱褶皱,如嵩山的铮铮铁骨,又如一本厚重的地质百科全书。古老、悠久的嵩山,其诞生、演化就是中原大地沧桑变迁的见证。嵩山以其丰

的设计，却成为最为匠心独运的应用。《风中少林》每次拉开帷幕，舞美中它得到激赏最多。在感叹"天籁难为"之时，你我心中似乎感悟到了佛与山之间的某种默契。

"嵩高山者，莫位天中"，"而为万山之宗欤"。其南绕颍水，北依黄河，东西延绵百里，重峦叠嶂，气势磅礴，突兀中州，极天柱地。屹立中原的巍巍嵩山从远古走来，在见证中原大地沧桑变迁的历程中，每一道记忆的皱纹，都留存着令人神往的奥秘；它的每一座山峰、每一道山脊，都在与风雨的抗争中，成为力与美的展示。太室如龙眠，雄伟壮美；少室如凤舞，险峻秀丽。当我们置身群峰之间，就会

Sanhuangzhai Suspension Bridge at Mount Song　嵩山三皇寨吊桥

富的地质文化内涵，独特的地质构造和珍稀的地质遗迹，在2004年被评审为世界地质公园。

World Geopark of Mount Song　嵩山世界地质公园

试图理解嵩山"崇高"、"岳山"的含义，就极力想去理解它
能成为皇帝祭天封禅、忏悔赎罪之圣地的奥秘，想去探究它
成为儒、释、道三教荟萃、相聚对话之福地的因果，嵩山是
东方的奥林匹斯圣山，有着我们永远读不完的神奇奥妙。

　　嵩山之为五岳之尊，除却博大精深的文化积淀和形胜之
势外，亦在于嵩山阅尽沧桑的地质构造。嵩山壁立千仞，褶
皱千层，尖棱如锥，危若累卵，纹路旋转，悬崖险峭，峡谷
幽深。山石奇特怪异，石色斑斓，赤橙黄绿青白紫应有尽有，
大自然的鬼斧神工令人感怀惊叹。

　　嵩山，是一本用石头写成的天书。

少室山　Shaoshi Mountain

The huge curtains are hanging onto the front of the stage. The rock cliffs on the curtains and the mountain cliffs at the back of the stage set each other off spectacularly, looming through the curtains, aloof and steep with a slight mystery.

On the stage of *Shaolin in the Wind*, imposing and powerful with extraordinary splendour, strength and profound meanings are conveyed by the mobile pagoda forest, the tilting torii and the lodging stone lions, making one feel personally on the scene, bestowed with profound understanding of life, thus unwilling to return. And the most stirring scene is doubtlessly the massy rocks and cliffs in the deep rear of the stage.

This is just an ordinary rock taken from Mount Song and the only natural setting on the stage, yet it turns out to be the most eye-catching work with the finest ingenuity. Every time when the curtains are drawn open to perform *Shaolin in the Wind*, it always wins more praise than any other settings. While marveling at the superb craftsmanship, the audience seemingly perceive some perfect harmony between Buddha and the mountain.

Related Links
Lofty and Steep Mount Song

The stratum structure of Mt. Song possesses immeasurable significance in the world geological contrastive study. There are numerous rare and non-regenerating geological relics in this area, incorporating typicality, rarity and systematic structure into an organic whole, thus making it an ideal place to research on the laws of evolvement of the earth's crust, and to trace the evolving history of the earth. Within an area of less than 400 km², it is famous for its complete and sequential outcrops of stratigraphic section and the boundaries of angular unconformities formed by 3 Precambrian tectonic movements and there are found outcrops of the Archean, Proterozoic, Palaeozoic, Mesozoic and Cenozoic eras. The boundaries of angular unconformities were shaped by three Precambrian tectonic events. These were the Songyang movement (2.5 billion years ago) ,the

Standing in the Central-China Plains, Mt. Song over-shadows other mountains in China. With Yinghe River flowing in its south, the Yellow River running in its north, Mt. Song extends from the east to the west, winding its way for a hundred miles, majestic and lofty, standing towering in central China.

The lofty Mt. Song stands towering in the Central-China Plains from remote antiquity. It is the most telling witness for the historical changes in the Central-China Plains. Intoxicating and profound mystery exists in every wrinkle of memory in it. Every peak and every ridge of it have become a wonderful display of beauty and strength, braving wind and rain. Taishi Mountain sleeps like a dragon, grand and magnificent; Shaoshi Mountain dances like a phoenix, steep and elegant. When we place ourselves in these mountains, we are eager to understand why it could be a sacred place for emperors to pay tribute to gods in the heaven, a holy land for confession and atonement, and to probe into the reason why this area is also an assembly point of three major religions in China—Buddhism, Confucianism and Taoism—and one of the birthplaces of China's ancient culture. Mt.

Zhongyue movement (1.8 billion years ago), and the Shaolin movement (543 million years ago). With these tectonic disturbances, stratigraphic sections of Archean, Proterozoic, Mesozoic, and Cenzoic eras were brought together. It is generally known as the "geo-family of five generations" and is a textbook of geological history. On February 13, 2004, Mt. Song successfully passed the examination and appraisal and was chosen as the World Geopark owing to its peculiar geological structure and its rare geological relics.

Song is the holy Olympus for the Orient, richly laden with endless subtleties and mysteries. One can hear the sound of ancient bells and drums, and view many historical and religious remains such as Buddhist temples and pagodas, Taoist temples and ancient academies of classical learning. The geological and cultural sites form a delightful contrast, making the area an ideal tourist attraction.

Ranking among the Five Sacred Mountains in China, Mt. Song boasts its age-long geological structure, in addition to its profound cultural accumulation and majestic loftiness. Mt. Song is famous for its lofty stature, intrinsic creases, prick-like sharp ridges, extremely precarious slopes, eddying grains, steep cliffs and deep and remote gorges. The mountain stones are exotic and grotesque, gorgeously beautiful with all kinds of colors including red, orange, yellow, green, blue, white and purple. The superb craftsmanship in nature is strikingly marvelous.

Mt. Song is a book from heaven carved with stones.

Taishi Mountain 太室山

风中 SHAOLIN: DANCING IN THE WIND 动少林

CHAPTER FOUR 肆

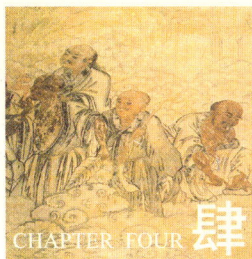

一束灯光渐亮，一身袈裟的慧山大师缓缓步出，空旷、悠远的钟声响起，我们也可以听见大地深处的梵唱……

我们来自何处？我们现在何方？

灯影婆娑，勾栏画肆，俗世画卷里我们可以看见名伶天元、素水夫妻相对起舞，一支花翎舞尽素水婀娜妖娆，一方丝帕写就天元蜜语万千。好一幅诗情水墨，好一曲柔意浅唱。

┤ 相关链接 ├

楚河汉界

由郑州西北古荥迤逦前行，濒临黄河有古称广武山倚立。它东邻荥阳古城，西面不远处便是天下险关虎牢关（或称汜水关）。广武山恰好处于黄土高原和黄河中下游平原的交界处，几千年前这里是由平原进入西部的交通枢纽和战略要地，自然也就成为重要的军事关隘。

Hulao Pass　虎牢关

悠然变幻，呼啸的风声伴着肃然的合唱……

诡秘、狰狞的"鬼眼独"拖着沉重的绳索向舞台深处走去，舞台上的红光黑影也就告诉我们这片土地上灾难的来临。冰冷黑色的杀掠将天元和素水所有绚烂的梦想、玫瑰般的甜蜜撕裂窒息。

秦始皇横扫六合时，占据广武山，在山上建立敖仓，作为消灭魏、韩、齐的大本营。隋炀帝开运河、下江南，就是先通过广武之间的鸿沟，由这里东下入汴河，再进入运河。

这里至今还横亘着秦时的古荥阳城，它和汉时的皇家冶铁遗址比邻相望，尽管这两处国家文物保护单位声名远播，尤其是冶铁遗址更是世界冶铁史上的圣坛，可当地百姓口碑相传更多的还是纪信将军和两千多年前的楚汉之战，楚汉相争的历史风云千百年来一直弥漫在广武山上空。

Statue of General JiXin in the Town God's Temple in Zhengzhou　郑州城隍庙纪信像

　　已经模糊了，历史在书写"逐鹿中原"的笔迹之时，是天下杀伐的英雄篇章，还是生灵涂炭的腥风血雨？⋯⋯翻开历史，从黄帝与炎帝的阪泉之战、黄帝与蚩尤的涿鹿之战开始，这里的四季在刀光剑影中轮回，这里的每一寸土地都叠印着征战的铁蹄：敖山晋楚杀声雷动，广武风传百战之声，楚河汉界从没挡住蜂拥的兵车箭船，虎牢关前白骨幽魂写下易逝的胜负⋯⋯

Chu River and Han Boundary　楚河汉界

　　两千多年前的那场荥阳之战，是刘项角逐最后的大决战。公元前205年，刘邦出函谷关东进，兵败困守荥阳。大将纪信出城假扮刘邦诈降，刘邦借机逃出。愤怒的项羽将纪信焚死于城下，这一把火成就了兴汉第一臣纪将军的忠烈功名，也给郑州这座城市造就了一位护城佑民的城隍神。人们在纪将军殉身之处修建衣冠冢，千年香火祭奠，至今庙墓仍存。郑州城内供奉纪信的城隍庙也是保存最为完好的古建筑群。

Town God's Temple of Zhengzhou　郑州城隍庙

　　映着冲天的火光，满台的绳索构成天罗地网。逃亡的脚步躲不过入侵者的追杀，文弱的伶人敌不过强寇的魔掌，逃难中重伤的天元和妻子素水失散……

　　倒伏的石狮发出无声的悲鸣。

　　美丽在掠杀中飘零，安宁在杀戮中消失，一个和平的梦想再次遍体鳞伤……

　　两年后，刘邦重整旗鼓，由成皋东进至广武，在鸿沟西筑城，即今日之汉王城。项羽在鸿沟东筑城，即今日之霸王城。以后的故事中国人耳熟能详，鸿沟相持，是悲情英雄项羽的覆灭之战。而刘邦于公元前202年正月，在汜水之阳（即与广武相对的大伾山）即皇帝位，开始了汉王朝的新纪元。也许是为了纪念，人们在象棋盘上划出"楚河汉界"延续捉对厮杀，为你述说历史沧桑，英雄悲歌……

　　仰天长叹之时，慧山大师从远处走来，橘黄的身影抚慰着善良的心愿。

　　少林就是这样走来的。少林寺在中国历史传奇中始终扮演着扶危济困、匡扶正义的角色。透过历史的云烟，我们可以寻觅少林僧人历次救国家于危难、救苍生于水火的传奇：

少林寺

　　天下第一名刹，禅宗祖庭，少林武术的发源地。

　　北魏孝文帝太和十九年（495年），印度高僧跋陀由西域落迹传教，深居嵩山，孝文帝为其在少室山北麓的茂密丛林之中敕建少林寺，"少林寺"因此得名。北魏孝明帝孝昌年间（525—527年），释迦牟尼大弟子摩诃迦叶的第二十八代佛

Picture of Dharma　达摩像

十三棍僧救唐王,紧那罗变形退红巾,月空棍僧抗倭寇,三奇和尚镇山陕……一个个张扬着正义与豪情的故事,让少林的名字气吞山河、横扫古今……

到了上世纪80年代,电影《少林寺》又给了全国人民重新温习历史的机会:

"少林、少林,有多少英雄豪杰都来把你敬仰;

少林、少林,有多少神奇故事到处把你传扬……"

歌曲唱响大江南北,点燃了无数男女热血英雄的梦想。

观众知道任何故事到了危难的节点之时,只要少林寺的形象出现,正剧就开始了……

我们有理由期待。

在人们苦苦的期盼中,它总算来到天元身旁。在慧山大师张开慈悲之怀的一瞬,悸动的,是我们善良的希冀。

Film Posters of "Shaolin Buddhist Monastery" 《少林寺》电影海报

徒达摩来到嵩山少林寺,将印度大乘佛教和中国儒家思想融合,创立禅宗。达摩被佛教界尊奉为中国禅宗的初祖,少林寺也被奉为中国佛教的禅宗祖庭。

少林寺以禅宗和武术并称于世,隋唐时期已具盛名。宋代,少林武术已自成体系,风格独绝,史称"少林派",成为中国武术派别中的佼佼者。

A beam of light is shining gradually. The cassocked Great Master Hui Shan slowly appears on the stage. The bell begins to ring, the sound remote and hollow. We can also hear songs in Sanscrit in the remote depths of the land...

Where were we from?

Where are we now?

The shadows of the lights are dancing on the stage. In the painting pavilion and the theatrical loft, Tian Yuan and Su Shui are dancing trippingly. The dance with graceful and long pheasant tail feathers gives the fullest display to Su Shui's graceful and enchanting carriage. A silk handkerchief embodies Tian Yuan's passionate love for her. What a perfect scene of poetic charm and tender affection!

The scene on the stage suddenly changes. Grave and solemn chorus rises, accompanied by howling wind. The surreptitious and ferocious "one-eyed ghost" is dragging heavy cord toward the deep rear of the stage, indicating the impending disaster. The cold and dark slaughter shatters all the flowery dreams of Tian Yuan and Su Shui, lancinating and suffocating their rosy sweet love.

All the scenes have become obscure. When history

Related Links
Boundary Between Chu and Han

Located near Guxing county to the northwest of Zhengzhou city, and close to the Yellow River, stands Guangwu mountain, lofty and majestic, adjacent to the ancient city of Xingyang in the east, and the hardly accessible strategic Hulao Pass(also called Sihe River Pass) in the west. Guangwu mountain is rightly located at the joint of the Loess Plateau and the plains at the middle and the lower reaches of the Yellow River. Several thousand years ago, it was a hub of transportation as well as a strategic highland, thus naturally becoming a critical military pass.

When Emperor Yingzheng (the first emperor of the Qin Dynasty) united and ruled the whole country in ancient China, he held the pass at Guangwu mountain, erecting storehouses, making it the base camp to annihilate the states of Wei, Han and Qi. When Emperor Yangdi in the Sui Dynasty dug the canal and went to the

records the picture of "chasing the deer in the Central-China Plains" (trying to seize control of the whole empire), is it a heroic epic of killing and cutting, or a period of foul wind and blood rain, plunging the people into an abyss of misery? Many events are laid bear in historical records, including the battle at Banquan between the Yellow Emperor and the Fire Emperor (also called Shen Nong, meaning Spirit Farmer; both of them are legendary rulers in ancient China), and the battle at Zhuolu in which the Yellow Emperor defeated Chi You. The four seasons repeat themselves in the glint and flash of daggers and swords here. Each and every inch of this land has been superimposed with the iron heels in battles and wars, which include the thunderous killing at Aoshan between the states of Jin and Chu, the drastic battles at Guangwu, the famous battle between the territories of the states of Chu and Han as well as the unforgettable fighting in front of the Hulao Pass...

The flame is towering, and cord covering the stage is forming a tight encirclement. Brutal bandits invade and kill Tian Yuan and Su Shui all the way. They could hardly escape. The gentle and weak Tian Yuan suffers enough from hu-

south, he first passed the great gulf at Guangwu, and traveled through Bianhe river to reach the canal.

At present, the ancient city of Xingyang built in the Qin Dynasty still lies across this region, with the royal smeltery site of the Han Dynasty being its opposite neighbor. Although this place is famous for these two national cultural relics preservation units, especially for the smeltery site, which is regarded as the altar in the world smeltery history, it is unanimously praised by the local people for the Great General Ji Xin and the battle between the states of Chu and Han which was fought over 2,000 years ago. The historical influence of the grappling conflict between the states of Chu and Han has been permeating Guangwu county throughout thousands of years.

The battle fought at Xingyang over 2,000 years ago is the last decisive battle

miliation and is covered all over with cuts and bruises. He is seriously injured in his flee from the calamity. Unluckily, they are separated from each other...

The stone lions falling down to the ground are moaning sadly and silently.

Beauty is plundered away, peace is slaughtered and is vanishing, and the dream of peace is again shattered.

While the audiences are uttering sympathetic sighing, Master Hui Shan in orange robe is coming from afar, bringing the kind-hearted people a ray of hope.

Embodied in the Master is the Shaolin spirit. Shaolin monks have been playing the role of saving the country from danger, helping the people in poverty and danger, correcting the maladies of the times and promoting justice in the legends of Chinese history: Thirteen Shaolin monks fighting to capture Wang Shichong (self-appointed emperor of the Zheng state, a threat to the new dynasty of Tang) and rescue Li Shimin (king of the Qin state, later the second emperor of the Tang Dynasty), Master Zong Yin fighting against the armies of the Jin Dynasty, King Jinnaluo defeating Red Scarf Army, Master Yue Kong fighting against Japa-

in the grappling between Liu Bang and Xiang Yu. In 205 B.C., Liu Bang led his army out of Hangu Pass, marching eastward, but was defeated by Xiang Yu's army. He had to withdraw and stationed his army at Xingyang (the present-day Guxing county). Xingyang was tightly besieged like a metal pail by Xiang Yu's army. Having no forthcoming aid and no relief troops, Liu Bang's army was on the verge of destruction. Just at this critical juncture, the great general Ji Xin disguised himself as Liu Bang and pretended to surrender, which offered Liu Bang the chance to escape.The cooked and roasted duck has flown again. Out of aggravation, Xiang Yu burned Ji Xin to death outside the city wall. This grand deed brought to Ji Xin the fame of the best and the most loyal general for the establishment of the Han Dynasty, making him the town god to protect the town and the people in the city of Zhengzhou. People built a cenotaph on the spot of his sacrifice, holding memorial

nese pirates, Monk San Qi guarding the fortress, etc. Each story manifests the justice and lofty sentiments, making Shaolin Buddhist Monastery magnificent and famous through the history.

During the 1980s, the movie "Shaolin Buddhist Monastery" reminded people all over the country of the history of Shaolin Buddhist Monastery.

"Shaolin, Shaolin,

So many heroes admire you;

Shaolin, Shaolin,

So many stories sing high praises of you..."

This song hit the country quickly, and ignited the countless dreams of being heroes.

Whenever the image of Shaolin Buddhist Monastery appears at the moment of life and death, audiences all know that a heroic story will start.

Audiences are expecting...

Finally, Master Hui Shan extends his merciful hands towards Tian Yuan...

Notes:

1. Chi You is a belligerent and paramount leader of a clan in ancient China. In about 2700 B.C. Xuan Yuan (later called the Yellow Emperor), with the helps from other clans, fought a decisive battle with the united forces led by Chi You at Zhuolu (present day Huailai county in Hebei Province). Chi You, the leader of his alliance, was killed in the battle.

2. Chu is one of the Warring States into which China was divided during the Eastern Zhou period (770 B.C.-256 B.C.), occupying what is now Hubei and Hunan (esp. the former).

3. Jin is a state in the Zhou Dynasty, occupying parts of what are now Shanxi, Shaanxi, Hebei, and Henan.

ceremonies to worship him. The Town God's Temple in Zhengzhou is one of the best preserved ancient architecture complexes in China.

Two years later, in 203 B.C., Liu Bang rallied his army, marching from the east of Chenggao to Guangwu. He built a city on the west side of the great gulf, which is presently called the City of the King of Han. Xiang Yu built his city on the east side, which is now called the City of Hegemon King (the King of Chu, a title assumed by Xiang Yu, 232 B.C.-202 B.C.). There is a valley between them called the great gulf, or Guangwu gully. What follows is familiar to all the Chinese people: the confrontation between the two sides finally leads to the complete collapse of the army led by the heroic yet tragic Xiang Yu. In January, 202 B.C. on the Chinese lunar calendar, Liu Bang ascended the throne on the north of Sihe River (i.e. Dapi mountain opposite to Guangwu), opening a new era for the Han Dynasty. Probably in order to commemorate this event, the Chinese people play Chinese chess and rival with their opponents on a board on which "Chu River and Han Boundary" are drawn. Today when people climb up to the top of Guangwu mountain, they can't help recollecting historical events at the sight of the huge steles of the Two Cities of the King of Han and the Hegemon King. The cast iron horses seemingly crane their necks, neighing loudly, which often remind people of the elegy for the parting hero...

Shaolin Buddhist Monastery

It is called the "No.1 Famous Temple under Heaven", the "ancestral court of Ch'an Buddhism" and is generally regarded as the birthplace of Shaolin Martial Art.

During the reign of Emperor Xiaowen of the Northern Wei Dynasty in 495 A.D., an eminent Indian monk named Bhadra (also called Bada, Moha, or Buddha) came to Mt. Song after a long, arduous journey and settled there. The emperor ordered his men to build the temple for him in the dense forest at the north side of Shaoshi Mountain, and then named it Shaolin Buddhist Monastery (meaning "the temple in the forests of Shaoshi Mountain"). Later during the reign of Emperor Xiaochang(525 A.D.-527 A.D.), Dharma, the 28th patriarch of Ch'an Buddhism, who was instructed to transmit Dharma to China by Mahakashyapa (the 1st patriarch of Ch'an Buddhism), Sakyamuni's first disciple, came to the Shaolin Buddhist Monastery. By combining the Indian Mahayana and China's Confucianism, he created Ch'an Buddhism. So Dharma was addressed respectfully in the circle of Buddhism as the founder of China's Ch'an Buddhism and the Shaolin Buddhist Monastery ancestral court of Ch'an Buddhism.

Shaolin Buddhist Monastery has been well known for Ch'an Buddhism and its martial art since the Sui and the Tang Dynasties. In the Song Dynasty, Shaolin Kung Fu formed its own style and system, called "Shaolin Sect", and became an outstanding one among all martial art sects in China. In the Yuan and the Ming Dynasties, with over 2,000 monks, Shaolin Buddhist Monastery became a famous Buddhist temple home and abroad. However, since the middle of the Qing Dynasty, Shaolin Buddhist Monastery has declined gradually.

Though having experienced a lot of changes, there are still abundant cultural

relics remaining in Shaolin Buddhist Monastery. The Changzhu (meaning regular residential) yard is the main architecture complex which is located on the north bank of Shaoxi River. Currently, there also remain the mountain gate, the living rooms, the Snow Pavilion (also called the Dharma Pavilion), the White Robe Hall, the Hall of Thousand Buddhas, the Kshitigarbha Hall, the Hall of Heavenly Kings, the Daxiong Hall, and the Cangjing Pavilion (also called Dharma Hall) etc. The enormous mountain gate was constructed in the 13th calendar year of the reign of Emperor Yongzheng (1735 A.D.) in the Qing Dynasty. The three big characters "少林寺" (pronounced as *shaolinsi* in Chinese pinyin) on the board above the entrance gate were written by Emperor Kangxi of the Qing Dynasty. Behind the Cangjing Pavilion is the abbot's residence, which was taken as the temporary dwelling palace of Emperor Qianlong when he passed by Shaolin Buddhist Monastery on the way to Zhongyue Temple in 1750. Behind the abbot's residence is the Dharma Pavilion, also called the Snow Pavilion. Legend has it that the 2nd patriarch of Ch'an Buddhism named Shen Guang stood in the snow to demonstrate his determination of learning Buddhism. To the west of Shaolin Buddhist Monastery is the Tower Yard where two ancient pagodas still remain. These two pagodas were both built by monk Guang Qing of the Northern Song Dynasty in 1087. In the Pagoda Forest, there are 250 tomb pagodas made of bricks or stones, which were built from the Tang Dynasty to the Qing Dynasty. Another important building is "Chuzu (Progenitor) Hut" or the "Mianbi (sitting in meditation facing the wall) Hut", which was built in the Northern Song Dynasty. All these architectures possess pretty high value in respect of history, art and science.

Notes: Generally, Shaolin Buddhist Monastery refers to the Changzhu Yard, the prime building of the Shaolin Buddhist Monastery, which is the center for the abbot and deacons of the temple to live and hold Buddhism activities. Built adjacent to the mountain, the Changzhu Yard has seven buildings including the major ones along the middle line and several others on the wings, covering more than 30,000 square meters in total.

Aeroview of Shaolin Buddhist Monastery 空中俯瞰少林寺

少林寺建筑群图（①大雄宝殿／②藏经阁／③天王殿／④天王殿内雕塑⑤塔林／⑥初祖庵／⑦鼓楼）
Pictures of Building Complex in Shaolin Buddhist Monastery
① Daxiong Hall; ② Cangjing Pavilion; ③ Hall of Heavenly Kings;
④ Statues in Hall of Heavenly Kings; ⑤ Pagoda Forest;
⑥ Chuzu (Progenitor) Hut; ⑦ Drum Tower

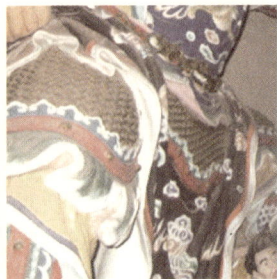

风中*舞*动少林
SHAOLIN:
DANCING
IN THE WIND

CHAPTER FIVE 伍

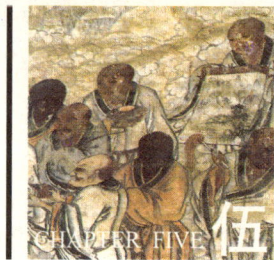

灯光暗转，及至渐亮时，我们进入到舞剧的第一幕，开始见到晨练的武僧和肃穆微笑的佛。

少林寺吸引俗世的红男绿女的魅力，其实在于禅、武、医三者一体博大精深的文化，更多还是在禅不在武。当冯双白先生为构思剧本而栖居少林寺聆听晨钟暮鼓之时，不知更多感悟的是什么？也许是和永信大师交谈的禅机，也许是禅、武、医集于一身的德建大师给予的灵感。不管怎样，我们有了以舞会禅、以舞述医、以舞融武的艰难的尝试。

相 关 链 接

少林禅医

少林禅医，是独特的医学流派。它在继承发扬中华传统医学理论的基础上，突出以"禅定"为基本法门，以呼吸、观想、气血、经络、脏象等学说为基本理论，运用"气化"、"导引"、"点摩"等基本手段进行诊断、治疗、调养。少林禅医的养生方式表现为：以功法为导，以医药为用，以禅修为髓，以提升生命力为归，其作用正在于激活潜能，锻炼脏腑，改造体质。多彩多姿的少林气功健身疗疾诸般功法，历代高僧珍藏秘传之丰富验方，结合超绝凡俗的武技功夫，或养生延寿，或济苦活人，成就无量功德。

少林医书 Shaolin Medical Books

　　少林医学探源至少追溯到建寺之初。据《少林武僧志》记载，禅师曾取嵩山草药补养、疗伤。北魏后期少林高僧洪遵和志刚，分别撰有《少林寺针灸秘抄》和《少林僧医宝囊》。隋代少林僧人子升善武好医，晚年撰述《摩穴秘旨》阐述气功医治，介绍人身六十八穴的部位、取法、疗效及配方，列举一百多种常见病的点穴治疗指要。"十三棍僧救唐王"中的寺主僧志操也是著名僧医，著有《少室僧针灸秘经集》和《跌打秘囊》等。唐代末年的福湖和尚善用针灸和草药，特别对止血、内瘀、厥症、危症等的治疗有独绝之处，撰有《少林伤科十大方》。宋代的洪温禅师擅长骨伤科，撰有《针后拔罐秘法》，觉远和尚对内科深有研究，有《少林寺内科神效录》传世。元代的惠定被尊为少林神医，著慧山将奄奄一息的天元抱进佛堂，气运丹田，天人合一。

少林众僧为天元发功疗伤，多少年来，普度众生的少林僧人一手仗剑行道，一手悬壶济世，心中萦绕的，总是无尽的禅意。

神奇禅医唤回了脱壳的魂魄，

无边法力复苏了生命的感觉……

天元醒来的时候，坐在佛祖前的蒲团上。当他舒展开曾经伤痕累累的四肢，欣喜地感觉到了生命的回归。尽管他不曾看到慧山师徒为他发功疗伤的情景，但他匍匐跪下时当然知道是少林给予了他新生，他身轻如燕的飞旋张扬的是生命的活力，更是少林医术的神奇。

少林医书中的人体经脉图
Drawings of Meridians and
Nervous System in Shaolin
Medical Books

有《少林骨科旨要》、《少林医家九散药谱》，惠矩的《针刺九十神穴》是针灸用穴的临床精华。明代著名的僧医有本明、幻休、正道等，清代较为著名的有湛举、寂盘、贞俊等。现代名僧德禅也是一代名医。

金朝末年，东林志隆出任少林寺住持，创建了少林药局，为僧俗治病。明代时少林寺还设医座、药局司等医僧官，同时还开设寺医学堂，少林医学秘方不断传入寺外，惠及大众，延至今日。近年少林寺将千百年来秘不外传的《易筋经》和《洗髓经》等珍藏的秘传武功医术，经过发掘、整理，历经三年编撰成《少林武功医宗秘笈》公布于世。

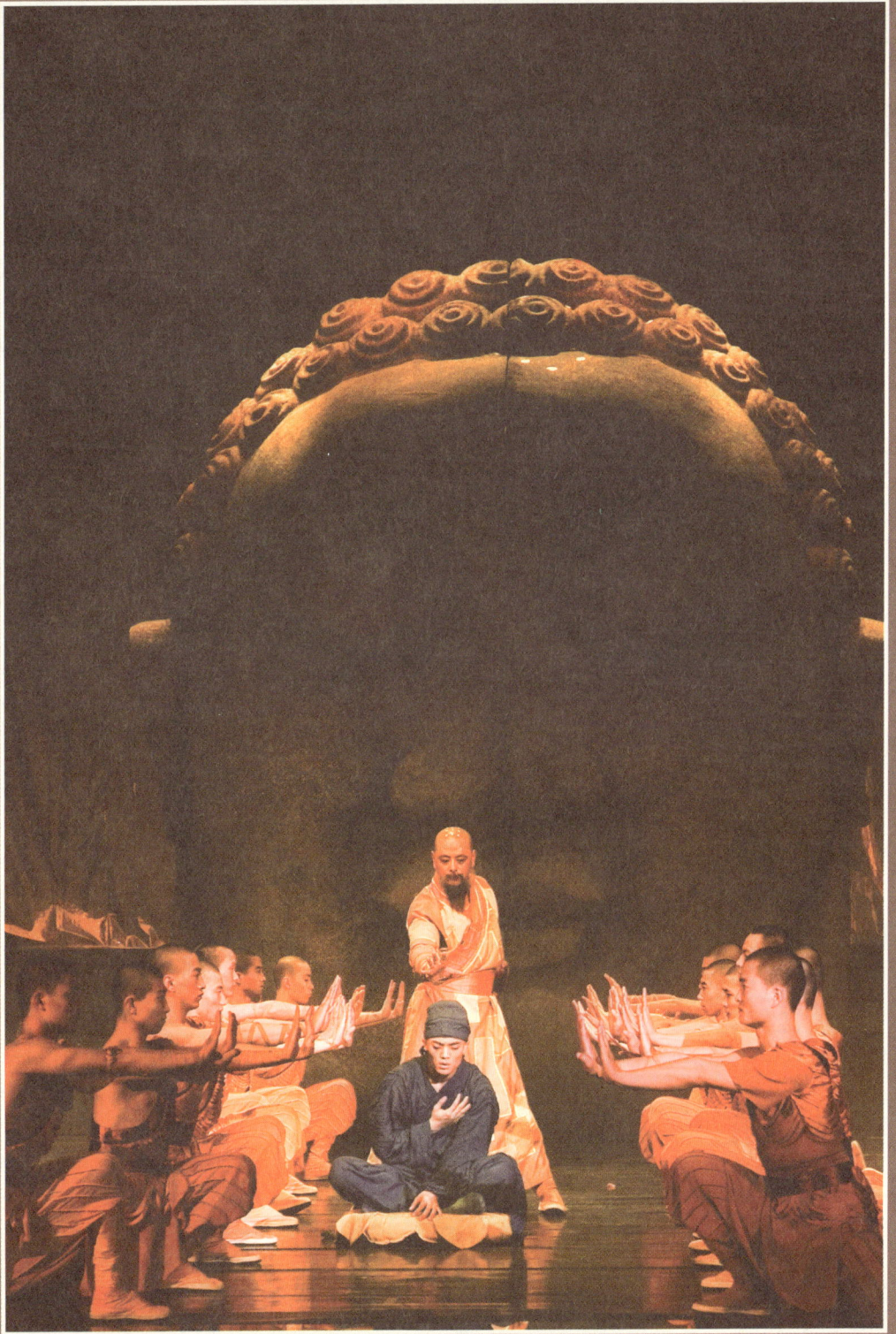

The light is turning dim. When it gradually becomes bright again, Act One of the dance drama begins. What come into the audiences' eyes first are the martial monks practicing Kung Fu in the morning, and the statue of the Buddha with holy smile.

It was the combination of Ch'an Buddhism, martial art and medical skills that attracted thousands of laymen. The core of its philosophy lies more in Ch'an Buddhism than martial art. On hearing the morning bells and evening drums in Shaolin Buddhist Monastery, what does Feng Shuangbai, the dramatist, come to realize when framing up the play? Was he inspired by the philosophy of Ch'an Buddhism while talking with Master Yong Xin, or was he enlightened by Master De Jian, a master of Ch'an Buddhism, martial arts and medical skills? Anyway, we've made a painstaking attempt to elaborate Ch'an Buddhism, martial arts and medical skills through dancing.

Master Hui Shan carries Tian Yuan at the verge of death into the hall and cures him with magic Shaolin medical skills.

Many other martial monks participate in curing Tian

Related Links
Shaolin Medical Skills

Shaolin medical skills have absorbed many concepts from Indian medical culture and Chinese medical culture, thus making a combination of the two sects after the practice of them for over two thousand years. They carry forward the theory of traditional Chinese medicine by making "meditation" the basic rules, using theories of breath, meditation, vital energy and the state of blood, main and collateral channels, and state of internal organs as its basic theory.

Shaolin medical skills teach people to conserve vital power by taking Kung Fu as the guide, medicine as the cure, meditation as the essence and strengthening vital power as the purpose. They aim at activating people's potential, strengthening their internal organs and building up their physiques. The combination of recipes carried down by eminent monks of different generations and the powerful

Yuan with Shaolin medical skills. For years, monks in Shaolin Buddhist Monastery help to deliver people from torment with Shaolin Kung Fu and medical skills.

With the magic martial medical skills, Tian Yuan comes to life again. Sitting on the rush cushion in front of the statue of the Buddha, Tian Yuan stretches his scarred body and is grateful that he is still alive. Although he doesn't witness how Master Hui Shan cures him, he clearly knows that it is Shaolin Buddhist Monastery that grants him a new life. The fact that he regains vigor and strength can testify the magic of the Shaolin medical skills.

Shaolin Kung Fu makes people live in longevity and in a healthy way.

Shaolin's Ch'an Buddhism philosophy advocates "strengthening people's health with their own internal force". Today, this concept accords more with the latest development of "activating people's potential" in the world and leads the international trend of active health-care. In order to sum up the special medical skills into a system, Shaolin Buddhist Monastery has made known to the public "*Yijinjing*" and "*Xisuijing*" which are the treasures of Shaolin Buddhist Monastery and have been kept secretly over hundreds of years. After three years of compiling and editing, the book entitled "Secrets of Medicinal Skills of Shaolin Martial Art" was published.

Notes:

The form of chi kung (breathing exercises) that Dharma invented during his nine year meditation in a natural rock cave located behind the Shaolin Buddhist Monastery is called Yijinjing (meaning "Exchange of Muscle Passages", or "Channel-changing Scripture", also written as Yi Gen Jing). And though Dharma certainly must have drawn upon Indian yoga in inventing Yijinjing, what he actually did was to combine his own internal Kung Fu theory with the already existing Chinese theory of chi kung, while taking the differences in Chinese physiology and physical environment into account.

Yijinjing is a very important part of chi kung, but there are still other forms of Shaolin chi kung in existence. Yijinjing is an internal exercise that makes the body almost indestructible, capable of withstanding tremendous physical force and even injury from knife stabbing.

In addition to Yijinjing, Dharma invented another type of chi kung called Xisuijing or "Essence of Bone Washing" ,an internal exercise designed to cleanse the body. A later Shaolin Monk called Fu Yu invented two other forms of Shaolin chi kung: Ba Duan Jin, meaning "Eight Section Brocade", an internal exercise practiced to make the body as soft and as flexible as cotton to increase healthiness, rejuvenation, and longevity, and Shi Da Gong Fa, meaning "Ten Great Skills" ,an internal exercise to make the body hard as iron, and a very important skill in developing hard chi kung breaking skills. What Yijinjing and the other forms of chi kung have in common is chi.

风中
SHAOLIN:
DANCING
IN THE WIND
动少林

CHAPTER SIX 陆

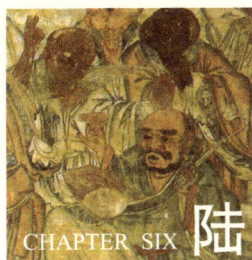

　　这一切都是在佛的安详笑意里进行的。

　　我们忘不了舞台上那尊大佛挂在嘴角的安宁神态,神秘笑意。

　　佛的笑是宽容的笑,慈悲的笑,爱怜的笑,开心的笑,指引的笑。佛祖拈花而笑,这一笑,世上一切妩媚、欢欣、狂喜乃至悲愤的笑都黯然失色。佛的笑,代表了无数的含义,又不代表任何具体含义。佛法无边,用任何的语言都无法解释,于是佛祖用了最简单的办法,微微一笑,就让他的

　　相 关 链 接

初祖达摩与二祖慧可

　　南朝梁武帝普通七年(526年),达摩为了弘扬大乘佛法,不辞艰险,航海来到中国,先到广州,次年到金陵,因与梁武帝萧衍论佛法所谈不契,于是决定渡江北行传法。行至江边,天色渐晚,浩瀚的江面上竟然不见一只可以横渡的舟船,菩提达摩双手合十,面对西方,口中喃喃:我自西来,深有密意,法若无生,我愿沉江,法若得兴,天助我也。说完,菩提达摩顺手摘下一枝芦苇扔进江流,他跃上芦苇,轻柔的芦苇竟令人不可思议地载着他一路顺风顺水,直向烟波浩渺的江心驶去……

达摩一苇渡江图　Drawing of Dharma's Sailing Across a River on a Leaf of Reed

弟子迦叶开悟。佛祖的笑，充满智慧，并且鼓励每个生灵都体会到他的智慧。

佛祖的安详是自我修炼而寻求的自由，更是仁慈、救赎的玄妙觉悟。

"他找到了自由，

他平静地思想，

平静地说话，

平静地行事，

他的心，充满安详。"

佛也许在那一刻对天元轻启了佛门，说："你要是自己的灯，是自己的避难所……小心看护你们的身体、情感、意识、心境和观念……"遍阅典籍，也许不如置身嵩山寻求与佛有着怎样的机缘。

对于历经苦难的天元来说，"少林"这两个字又有什么独特的魅力？当他跟着慧山大师和小沙弥游历少林的时候，心中肯定涌起了阵阵暖意。

达摩来到少林寺后，在嵩山一处幽深的洞窟，开始了长达九年的面壁坐禅。他相信，在这片广袤的大地上，终究会有一位坚定的禅者来继承他的衣钵。伴随往复生消的太阳和风雨，他不知道坐烂了多少蒲团，岁月将他高大的身影镌刻在洞中潮湿的石壁，他也得以超然，创立了禅宗。敬服达摩的毅力和崇高的佛学造诣，少林众僧遂诚心皈依禅学。

创业者的坚定与继承衣钵者的坚毅，有异曲同工之妙。在少林寺的立

达摩面壁图　The Feat of Cultivation and Meditation—Dharma Facing the Wall for Nine Years

穿过重重叠叠的院落，或许他也会在"三大殿"虔诚地敬上三炷清香，为失散的亲人、为在战火中飘摇的乡亲们祈福。

立雪亭、钟鼓楼、锤谱堂、塔林……在他身边梦幻般掠过，徘徊于一通通残断模糊的碑刻间，他也许在揣摩其中意蕴，忘却了人世的纷扰。

走进"深山藏古寺，碧溪锁少林"的清幽，置身"曲径通幽处，禅房花木深"的景象，天元那颗历经苦难的心，也沾上了几分禅机。遗憾的是，情牵着生死未卜的恋人，他无心欣赏自然景观与人文景观融为一体的宝刹风光，无法心绪宁静地思虑其间的义理。

立雪亭 Snow Pavilion

雪亭前，有这样一副对联："禅宗初祖天竺僧，断壁求法立雪人"。上联，讲来自天竺的达摩；下联，讲的是二祖慧可。

二祖慧可，俗名神光，是达摩的忠实追随者。深冬之夜，为求达摩传授佛法，神光彻夜立于达摩住所外的大雪之中，积雪没过双膝而不移。达摩伸手拂去神光周身的积雪，又敲碎他腿上的坚冰，冷漠地说：你还是回去吧，除非雪见红光。这时，只见空中一道寒光闪过，随着神光那柄腰刀的起落，他的手臂已经与躯体分离，殷红的鲜血喷洒在洁白的大地上。

达摩见此情景，为他献身佛教的赤诚所感动，传了衣钵，赐名慧可，是为禅宗二祖。据说，后代僧人感念二祖之坚，自此斜披袈裟，单掌施礼，延续至今。

眼前让天元眼花缭乱的少林武僧于洗衣、吃饭之间不经意显露的神奇武功，却更让他记起伶人天涯浪迹的生活，妻子婀娜曼妙的舞姿，夫妻相濡以沫的情爱。

天元辞别慧山，去尘世寻找离散的妻子，给少林寺留下一个存有悬念的背影。

慧可断臂求法
Hui Ke's Pursuit of Dharma, Standing in Red
Snow with His Arm Cut

The Buddha witnesses all these with his serene and amiable smile.

The calm and mysterious smile of the Buddha on the stage is unforgettable.

That is the smile of tolerance, mercy, benevolence, happiness and guidance. Any smile of charm, happiness, ecstasy or even grief will be overshadowed by such a smile. It embodies all but no specific meaning. The power of the Buddha is so overwhelming that no certain language can explain. In the simplest way, he enlightened his disciple only with this smile. His smile is full of wisdom and inspires his disciples and all the living creatures in this world.

His serene look comes from the freedom attained through self-cultivation and sudden realization of benevolence and salvation.

"He acquires freedom;

He thinks calmly,

Speaks calmly,

And acts calmly,

His heart is filled with serenity."

Maybe it is at that moment that the Buddha enlight-

Related Links
Bodhi Dharma and 2nd Patriarch of Buddhism—Hui-ke

In 526 A.D. during the reign of Emperor Wu of the Liang Dynasty, Bodhi Dharma came to China to preach Mahayana Buddhism. He arrived in Luoyang from India after passing through Guangdong and crossing the Yangtse River in Nanjing. He settled in the Shaolin Buddhist Monastery and gathered together a larger number of followers whom he taught the sutras of Ch'an Buddhism. It was said that Bodhi Dharma always sat quietly facing a wall, which was called "Facing a Wall in Meditation" and was the inevitable course and the elementary step for being a real Ch'an Buddhist. He sat in meditation in a cave on top of Shaoshi Mountain for nine years and his shadow was imprinted on the wall. He hence founded the Ch'an Buddhism. Admiring his perseverance and profound attainment , Shaolin monks were determined to be converted to Ch'an Buddhism.

ens Tian Yuan with Buddhist doctrine, telling Tian Yuan: "You should be the light illuminating your own way, and the shelter protecting yourself from being hurt. Take care of your body, your feeling, your consciousness, your mood and your concept..." No Buddhist sutra could be better than coming to Shaolin Buddhist Monastery in Mt. Song in person to experience Buddhism.

What is the special fascination of the two characters "Shaolin" to Tian Yuan who has experienced so many hardships? When he visits Shaolin Buddhist Monastery under the guidance of Master Hui Shan and other monks, what fills his heart must be a warm feeling.

Going through the different sections of the Changzhu yard, he might burn incense to pray for his separated relatives and his fellow villagers who are suffering from a great deal of disorder and turmoil.

The Dharma Pavilion, the Bell Tower and the Drum Tower, the Pagoda Forest flash by him just as in a dreamland. Wandering among the dilapidated stone tablet, he might speculate about the implications and forget the troubles of the world.

Great similarity could be found in the determination and perseverance of both the founding Patriarch and his disciples. Couplets can be found in the front of the Snow Pavilion: "First Patriarch of Ch'an Buddhism coming from India; Second Patriarch pursuing Dharma standing in red snow with his arm cut".

After Bodhi Dharma came to China, many Chinese Buddhist believers wanted to be his followers, and Shen Guang was the most prominent among all of them. In order to be a disciple of Dharma, Shen Guang always followed him whenever and wherever he went and served Dharma whole-heartedly. One night when Shen Guang stood outside waiting for Dharma's waking up, it began to snow, and it snowed heavily till daybreak. The next morning when Dharma woke up and opened his door, he found that the ground was covered with thick snow and a man, also white, was standing in snow. It was no other than Shen Guang. Shen Guang begged

Squats way into the depth of the hill,

The antique monastery desolate and yet tranquil;

Wandering along the meandering path,

Totally lost in the dense woods with inebriation.

Staying in the tranquility of Shaolin Buddhist Monastery, Tian Yuan begins to grasp the essence of Buddhism. However, his worry about his sweetheart distracts him from the splendid view of Shaolin Buddhist Monastery, and from the deep meditation of Buddhism.

The magic Shaolin Kung Fu is inadvertently exposed by the monks in their daily life of washing clothes, having meals etc. Their ordinary life reminds Tian Yuan of his wandering life as a tramp, the graceful dance of his wife and the sweet days he has spent with his beautiful wife.

He bids farewell to Master Hui Shan to look for his wife, leaving his receding figure to the Shaolin Buddhist Monastery.

but was rejected by Dharma who said: "It's impossible unless it snows red snow." On hearing this, Shen Guang immediately cut his left arm. Before long, the snow-covered ground turned red. Bodhi Dharma was greatly moved by Shen Guang's action of sincerity and loyalty, and finally agreed to accept him as his disciple and passed one of his Buddhist Instrument and the legacy on him as evidence, and also granted him a Buddhist name, "Hui-ke". After Dharma left the Shaolin Buddhist Monastery, Hui-ke became the second-Generation Patriarch (or the Second Ancestor) of Chinese Ch'an Buddhism.

风中
SHAOLIN:
DANCING
IN THE WIND
舞
动少林

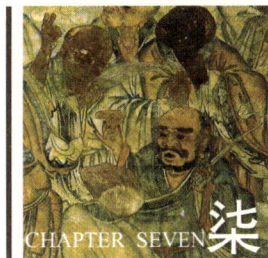

CHAPTER SEVEN 柒

天元走了，带着心中的感激，离开了佛门圣地。

天元走了，追寻失散的恋人，来到了繁华市井。

中原灯会，这是芸芸众生对新年景的祈福，是怀春男女的公开幽会，更是劳作一年后的激情狂欢。

这就是中原，这就是孕育着铁骨丹心的土地上的诗画风情：

灯笼挂起来了，锣鼓响起来了……

旱船摇起来了，高跷踩起来了……

相 关 链 接

嵩山社火

社火本是民间驱鬼酬神的仪式，后来逐渐演变成民间的娱乐形式，成为中国人集中狂欢的形式。

玩社火主要以各式各样的民间舞蹈为主。郑州地区的民间舞蹈丰富多彩，堪称中原民间舞蹈的代表，除常见的小黑驴、旱船、竹马、二鬼扳跌、张公背张婆、高跷、龙灯舞、挑经担、嵩山麒麟舞、老虎舞外，还有独具特色的嵩山英雄鼓舞、狮子舞、猩猩怪舞、独角舞、闹歌舞。

踩高跷 Dance of Walking on Stilts

龙灯舞、花篮舞、闹歌舞、老虎舞……舞得酣畅淋漓；

二鬼扳跌、挑经担、张公背张婆……闹得无所顾忌……

走进这中原民俗的大观园，再多的心思都会放下。戴上面具或涂上油彩，谁都不会甘做看客！

流离的素水也在灯会的人流中徘徊，用曼妙的花翎之舞倾诉对天元的思念。

缕缕思绪引来一色的青衣，一色的花饰，一色的清纯靓丽的民间少女同去翩跹起舞。五彩绚丽的雉鸡翎在手中婉转，那婀娜的舞姿之于这片土地，正如少女青色衣袂上那艳丽的流苏，从来不曾消失……

羽翎之舞是这阳刚之剧的阴柔慢板。它也许是这片土地的"天命玄鸟，降而生商"的鸟羽图腾遗风。商汤灭夏之后即命伊尹整《九韶》，创《大濩》，演《桑林》，集歌舞大成。

舞蹈郑州

郑州地区民间舞蹈源远流长。编成于春秋时期的我国最早的诗歌总集《诗经》，共305篇，其作品全部是配着乐舞演唱的歌词，经史家考证，"风"160篇，涉及河南的有109篇，从其中具有"郑风"特色的民间歌舞中，可看出郑州当时歌舞的繁盛景象。

在开凿于北魏的巩义石窟里，佛像两侧均刻有飞天、化生和莲花。弹琵琶、吹横笛的伎乐飞天，生动活泼，栩栩如生。

郑州城区出土的汉墓"官吏乐舞神话抹角空心砖"上部边缘有一排姿态优美的乐舞图，和"翘袖折腰舞"有相似之处，其特点是舞袖与下腰，舞女在腰间装饰一件环佩，飞扬的长袖绕至身后，这是汉时舞蹈的显著特点。

Images of Dance Drama Carved on Bricks in the Han Dynasty Unearthed in Zhengzhou　郑州出土的乐舞图汉砖

再早我们还可以上溯到黄帝的乐舞《云门》，黄帝在此
即位时天呈祥云，即以云为图腾，以云纪事，以云命官，作
乐舞祀之。也许黄帝的光泽依然，五千年后丙戌年拜祖大典
晴空天呈彩虹，祥瑞奇观被海内外一时传为美谈。

如今，演绎"郑风"的乐舞已经无从得知，好在还有凝
固的舞态，让我们用想象来还原历史，触摸这里歌舞的律
动——

细看打虎亭汉墓壁画，"宴饮百戏图"呼之欲出，汉墓
砖雕上，长袖缭绕、细腰倾折的巾袖之舞，姿态优美的乐舞

打虎亭汉墓舞乐图　Mural Paintings of Dance Drama in Dahuting Tomb of the Han Dynasty

现存于郑州博物馆的宋代"乐
舞宴饮画像铜镜"，上有跪坐的
主人和进物的侍者，并有人献
舞，一作舒袖舞，一作盘鼓
舞……

数年来，郑州出土的数千
块汉砖中，发现有数百块刻有
舞蹈动作造型的图画，如鼓舞、
盘舞等，还有新密打虎亭汉墓壁
画"宴饮百戏图"，都充分体现了
郑州地区汉代舞蹈艺术的风采。

乐舞宴饮画像铜镜
Images of Dance Drama Performed in the Court Feast Carved on the Broze Mirror of the Song Dynasty

图广袖飘飞。

巩义石窟的石刻飞天，飘带袅绕，体势流动，被誉为中国最美的石刻飞天。恰如李白诗：素手把芙蓉，虚步蹑太清。霓裳曳广带，飘拂升天行。

宋代的"乐舞宴饮画像铜镜"上，舒袖舞、盘鼓舞仪态万千。

这就是这片土地放飞心灵的风姿，

这就是这里的先民律动生命的形态。

伴着花开花落，

和着云飞浪涌……

Mural Paintings of Buddha in Gongyi Grottoes　巩义石窟飞天

郑州传统民间舞蹈主要有狮子舞、龙灯舞、旱船舞、小车舞、高跷舞等。

舞狮　Lion Dance

Dance of Rowing Land Boats　旱船舞

"去年元夜时，花市灯如昼。月上柳梢头，人约黄昏后。"

天元应当读过这首词，要不然，他不会在灯会如织的人流中，寻觅那熟悉的身影……

或许，这是他们游走江湖、飘零演艺的默契，早已许下的不期而遇的约定。

众里寻她千百度，蓦然回首，那人却在灯火阑珊处……

繁华市井，嵩山福地，狂喜的重逢变成甜蜜的约会。

在天元与素水缠绵、浪漫的遐想中，美丽的花屋从云端飘落，那一片片缤纷的花瓣，让人想起一首从《诗经·郑风》中飘来的诗：

溱与洧，方涣涣兮。士与女，方秉蕳兮。女曰"观乎？"士曰"既且"。"且往观乎？洧之外，洵讦且乐。"维士与女，伊其相谑，赠之

嵩山庙会

九龙潭庙会是嵩山别具特色的夜间庙会。嵩山地区人们敬奉的龙神主要是九龙圣母和九龙王，传说九龙圣母本是嵩山村姑，名叫康凤英，生育九龙，武则天加封其为九龙圣母。

农历五月十五举办的九龙潭九龙王庙庙会，规模盛大，影响遍及整个郑州地区。人们多在五月十四就上山进香，晚上在庙里或山坡上娱乐、休息。由于人们夜里上山要摸着山石登山，因此也称为"夜摸会"。五月十四夜色降临后，人们成群结队地涌向九龙王庙，一路人声鼎沸，灯火辉煌，在缭绕的香雾中，香客用黄裱纸折叠莲花，用金箔折叠元宝，焚香叩拜，吟唱经歌。最吸引人的是九龙圣母殿附近，人们在鼓、镲、笙、锣、板胡伴奏下，轮

以芍药。

　　这是《溱洧》勾画的郑国的青年男女相约到溱洧河畔踏春郊游，互诉心曲，暗送情物的情景。春水涣涣，碧波荡荡，春心也荡漾。他们在习习春风中，喁喁情语，互赠芍药，顾盼之间，情意绵绵。这世界东方的溱洧之畔，不就是西方人歌咏的伊甸园吗？

　　好一座美得让人心动的花屋，好一个舞得令人心醉的情梦，古老的"郑风"，就是最好的注释。

庙会上的戏曲表演
Opera Performance in Temple Fair

挑经担舞
Dance of Tiaojingdan (carrying the load of
Buddhist sutras)

番演唱曲剧、豫剧、河南坠子、河洛大鼓等，青年男女还随着节拍翩翩起舞，把庙会的气氛不断推向高潮。

　　九龙潭庙会是嵩山地区最有特色的庙会，是麦收后的庆祝会，是祈求九龙圣母和九龙王降雨以保佑秋季收成的祈雨会，是请九龙圣母和九龙王保佑全家平安、幸福的祈福会，是男女青年趁纳凉之机谈情说爱的甜蜜会。

郑 风

"郑风"是当时郑州地区的民歌,《诗经·郑风》所收的21首民歌中,竟有15首是情歌。2500年前的郑国人,对爱情的独钟让后人望而生叹。他们追逐爱情的热烈,恪守爱情的纯真,他们把爱洒向广袤的田野,撒向生活的各个角落,甚至于政治品德、社会交往,也都可以用爱的歌声来表达,其野性、率直让今天矜持的郑州人汗颜。

据《礼记》记载,古郑州地区,仲春二月,男女太牢,祀于神媒。青年男女踏青、郊游的溱洧河畔,成了他们相识相爱的伊甸园。春天来了,郑国的东门外成了青年人的自由王国,郑国的春天也因年轻人而更加美丽:

"出其东门,有女如云。虽则如云,匪我思存。缟衣綦巾,聊乐我员。

出其闉阇,有女如荼。虽则如荼,匪我思且。缟衣茹藘,聊可与娱。"

"有女如云"、"有女如荼",描绘出一幅美妙的风俗画卷。郑国的习俗,仲春二月,青年男女出游,要在城外、河边尽情享受大自然给予的爱,相互交往,毫无顾忌。他们把春天当作"神媒",青年人有了相识相爱的自由天地。"有女如云",俊俏的小伙便可在人群里穿来穿去,寻找自己欣赏的"素衣绿巾",倾吐相识相爱之情。

郑国的诗歌不仅在民间传唱,即使在官方交往中,也经常用诗歌来表达感情。公元前526年,晋国的使臣韩宣子出使郑国。春风和煦的日子,郑国的六位大臣在郊外为他送行。借着春风,大家诗兴大发。韩宣子请大臣都赋诗一首,郑国的子美首先吟诵了《野有蔓草》:

"野有蔓草,零露泞兮。有美一人,清扬婉兮。邂逅相遇,适我愿兮。

野有蔓草,零露瀼瀼。有美一人,婉如清扬。邂逅相遇,与子偕臧。"

良辰美景,邂逅丽人,一见钟情便携手走向芳林深处,这是多么浪漫的爱情。郑国的大臣把它献给晋国的使臣,纯洁的爱情化为真挚的友谊。韩宣子十分理解,郑晋更加友好。

Poetic Drawings in *Book of Odes* · *Odes of Zheng* · *Zhen and Wei*　《诗经·郑风·溱洧》诗意图

Tian Yuan leaves the sacred place of Buddhism with hearty appreciation, heading for the bustling and prosperous downtown to look for his lover who was separated from him and lost touch with him.

Lantern Fair of the Central-China Plains is a time and place for people to pray for a good harvest in the following year, for girls and boys to date their sweethearts and also for people to enjoy themselves unrestrainedly after a year's hard work.

This is the Central-China Plains, a large piece of land with beautiful scenery which can breed faithful and unyielding heroes:

The lanterns are hanging high; the drums are beaten hard...

Some people are performing the dance of rowing land boats (a model boat used as a stage prop in traditional folk dances); some are walking on stilts...

All kinds of folk dances are performed rapturously, including Dragon Lantern Dance, Flower Basket Dance, Tiger Dance, and Merry Singing Dance...

Comic dances are played freely without scruple, in-

Related Links
Shehuo (Traditional Festivities) in Mount Song

Shehuo, the traditional festivities in Mt. Song, originally a folk ceremony of exorcising evil ghosts and offering sacrifice to gods, has gradually evolved into a type of entertainment among the people. Playing Shehuo mainly refers to performing all kinds of folk dances. The folk dances in the region of Zhengzhou are rich and colorful, well representing the folk dances of the Central-China Plains. Apart from some common folk dances such as Little Black Donkey, Land Boat, Bamboo Horse, Erguibandie (wrestling of two ugly ghosts), dance of Old Zhang carrying his wife on his back, Stilts, Dragon Lantern Dance, Tiaojingdan, Mt. Song Unicorn Dance, and Tiger Dance, there are some other regional folk dances such as Dance of Mt. Song Hero Beating Drums, Lion Dance, Gorilla Monster Dance, Unicorn Dance and Merry Singing Dance.

cluding Erguibandie (wrestling of two ugly ghosts, a folk dance in which one person with some props performs the fighting of two ugly ghosts), Tiaojingdan (carrying the load of Buddhist sutras, originating from the story of Xuanzang, a monk of the Tang Dynasty who is famous for his west trek voyage to get Buddhist sutras and also renowned for his translations of Buddhist sutras from Sanskrit into Chinese, a dance played to show people's worship for Buddha), and dance of Old Zhang carrying his wife on his back...

Whoever visits the grand view garden of folk custom in the Central-China Plains would be unwilling to be just an onlooker. And he would like to put away his worries and cares in life, put on a mask or paint his face with grease-paint to join the merry dancers and singers.

Su Shui, drifting from place to place, homeless and miserable, is wandering among the throng of the fair, and is dancing with graceful and long pheasant tail feathers to manifest her missing to Tian Yuan.

Her feeling attracts a group of pure and beautiful civilian maidens in black clothing and with the same colorful

Mt. Song Shehuo can be classified into Polite Shehuo and Martial Shehuo. Polite Shehuo includes such folk dances as Bamboo Horse, Stilts, Merry Singing Dance, Land Boat, Big-head Child, Pigsy Carrying His Wife on His Back, etc. Both folk dances of Big-head Child and Pigsy Carrying His Wife on His Back are performed with masks. It looks like there are two people performing Pigsy Carrying His Wife on His Back, but in fact there is only one actor performing with props like the lower body of the wife and the upper body of Pigsy. Actors engaged in Polite Shehuo need making up for three purposes: firstly, because of the totem cult handed down from the earliest ancestors, people want to show their worship for the deities and ghosts by making up; secondly, with masks and painted face, actors can perform free from inhibition without the embarrassment of being recognized; at last, making up can make the characters they perform more distinctive.

decoration to dance together with her. The dance with graceful and long pheasant tail feathers is replete with elegance
and beauty, just like the bright tassel on the maidens'
sleeves, which has never vanished.

The dance with graceful and long pheasant tail feathers adds some mildness to the virility of the dance drama.
It represents the totem of plume of Zhengzhou area, for as
described in *Book of Odes*, a holy bird is commissioned by
god in the heavens to descend to the this world and give
birth to the Shang Dynasty. When the king of the Shang
Dynasty wiped out the Xia Dynasty, he had Yiyin collate
Nine Shao, create *Da Huo*, and had *Sang Lin* performed. We
can even trace further back to the dance drama *Gate of
Clouds* in the reign of the Yellow Emperor. When the Yellow
Emperor ascended the throne, there were auspicious clouds
in the sky; hence clouds were taken as a totem, used as the
sign of accounts and as the title for officials, and sacrifices
were offered to clouds in the form of dance. It is thought to
be the glory of the Yellow Emperor that resulted in the auspicious scene of rainbow 5,000 years later when the memorial ceremony is held for the Yellow Emperor in Xinzheng,

Compared with Polite Shehuo, Martial Shehuo, such as Gorilla Monster Dance
and Lion Dance, is a better manifestation of the fact that Shaolin Buddhist Monastery is the birthplace of Wushu (martial art). For performing Gorilla Monster Dance,
some martial artists wearing the gorilla-like clothes imitate the actions of a gorilla
to fight with each other, such as *Xingyi Quan* (pinyin for Shape and Intention boxing).
Among many kinds of performance in Lion Dance, the most surprising and wonderful show is a dance called "A Lion Climbing Up the High Mountain". First of all,
hundreds of benches are piled up and tied to form "a mountain" which is over 10
meters high, then "a lion" begins to climb "the mountain" while listening to the
sound of firecrackers and fireworks. "The lion" is usually performed by three martial artists, one of them, who is light and nimble, being the head of "the lion", and
the other two strong men in lion-skinned clothes being the body. With one of the

which has been widely passed on with approval both at home and abroad.

Nowadays, we are in no position to enjoy the dance drama elaborating *Odes of Zheng*, but we fortunately have these dances in written documents and in drawings, which help to reproduce history in our mind.

Looking closely at the mural painting in Dahuting (meaning "pavilion for hunting tigers") tomb of the Han Dynasty, we enjoy the pictures, which vividly depict unique acrobatics being played in the court feast. Flying Apsaras (angels) carved on the stone relief in Grottoes Temple in Gongyi county of Henan Province are praised as the most beautiful flying Apsaras in China, who are "cherishing the beauty of lotus, and wandering softly in the holy land; with fasciae hanging from their colorful clothing, they are flying to heaven" as described in Li Bai's poem.

Carved on the bronze mirror of the Song Dynasty is the dance performed in the court feast, dancers with unfolding sleeves and others dancing with drums performing in all their glory.

All these demonstrate the open-mindedness and the

two strong men holding his waist, "the lion head" will imitate the expressions and actions of a lion, such as its anger, surprise, standing, jumping, and "the body" will cooperate with him.

The performance of "the lion" on the top of "the mountain" is the most dangerous and exciting part of the show, in which "the lion" usually catches the ground merely with its fore legs or its hind legs, and the audience will be excited and frightened with its prancing, jumping and rolling. Sometimes two "mountains" will be piled up side by side and connected with one rope or two ropes, representing "the withered rattan between two mountains", and "the lion" will walk on "the rattan". Without the consummate skill of flying trapeze, the actors would hardly be competent to accomplish this task. "The lion walking through the valley" is the most exciting show of Lion Dance and usually the highlight of a lantern fair as well as a temple fair.

civilization of this land.

This is the way the ancestral people demonstrated their pattern of life which has been passed down from generation to generation with the passage of time.

Last year at the Lantern Festival,

The lanterns in the flower market were bright as day;

When the moon mounted to the tops of the willows,

Two lovers dated after dusk.

Tian Yuan might have read this *ci* (classical poetry conforming to a definite pattern). Otherwise, he wouldn't search for the figure of his beloved in the throng.

Maybe this is the constancy of belief held by them when they depart, that they will have a chance to reencounter.

Hundreds and thousands of times, for her he searched in chaos, suddenly, he turned by chance, to where the lights were waning, and there she stood!

The busy section of the town, blissful land of Mt. Song may become an ideal place for reunion.

When Tian Yuan and Su Shui are lost in fantastic and romantic reveries, beautiful flowers fall down from the sky. The petals of the flowers remind people of a song from *Book*

Folk Dance of Zhengzhou District

Folk dance of Zhengzhou district boasts a long history. *Book of Odes* compiled during the Spring and Autumn Period is the oldest collection of Chinese poetry. It is made up of 305 songs, odes and hymns, all of which are lyrics used in songs to accompany music and dance. The folk dance, characterized with the style of *Ode of Zheng*, well reflect the prosperity and richness in the dances popular in Zhengzhou in that period.

Carved in the Northern Wei Dynasty, statues of Buddha in Gongyi Grottoes are quite lively and vivid with the merry performing of flying Apsaras (angels) and lotus in high relief on both sides.

Unearthed in Zhengzhou proper, a hollow brick in a Han tomb is carved with a picture of dance with accompaniment along its upper sides. The picture is char-

of Odes ·Odes of Zheng:

> The Zhen and Wei,
>
> Now present their broad sheets of water.
>
> Ladies and gentlemen,
>
> Are carrying flowers of valerian.
>
> A lady says, 'Have you been to see?'
>
> A gentleman replies, ' I have been '.
>
> 'But let us go again to see.
>
> Beyond the Wei,
>
> The ground is large and fit for pleasure.'
>
> So the gentlemen and ladies,
>
> Make sport together,
>
> Presenting one another with small peonies.

The "Ode of Zhen and Wei" depicts the scene of courting of young lovers in the State of Zheng. They give each other small peonies as presents in a gentle breeze. Isn't the bank of the rivers of Zhen and Wei the Garden of Eden for the Orient as often extolled in the Western eulogies?

What beautiful flowers! What fascinating reveries! *Odes of Zheng* offers the best interpretation.

---

acterized by sleeve-waving and waist-bending, which are popular in the Han Dynasty.

Restored in Zhengzhou Museum, the Bronze Mirror carved with Dance Performed in the Court Feast presents a picture of feast and performance, with a sitting master, a servant offering food, a dancer with unfolding sleeves and another dancing with a drum.

For years, hundreds of bricks unearthed from Han tombs in Zhengzhou are carved with pictures showing dancers' posture and movement. All these reveal excellent dancing skill in the Han Dynasty in Zhengzhou district.

Traditional folk dance in Zhengzhou district includes mainly Lion Dance, Dragon Lantern Dance, Rowing Land Boat, Handcart Dance, Dance of Walking on Stilts and so on.

Dragon Lantern Dance: The skeleton of dragon for performance mainly consists of bamboo strips or sticks, wrapped with paper or cloth, and then painted in green, yellow and red. Sticks are attached to the dragon at intervals for the convenience of performance. The leading dancer holds a spider-like ball. Generally speaking, there are lights in both the dragon and the ball so that when performed at night, both the dragon and the ball are shining. When performing Dragon Lantern Dance, drums, gongs and suona horns are necessary for the sake of livening things up. Dragon Lantern Dance is often played at night and is quite striking.

Rowing Land Boat: The cast of the dance usually consists of female passengers and a boatman or several boatmen. When performing, each does things in his/her own role. The performance imitates basic movements of rowing boats in water such as setting sail, sailing, overturning the land boat, and striking water with paddles.

Handcart Dance: It is often performed by two people, an old man who pushes the cart and an old lady who sits on the cart. Sometimes a male dancer may play a reversed role as an old lady. Handcart dance reveals a certain plot, and dancers' movements mainly include lifting the cart, moving the cart, supporting the cart, running at high speed, running at low speed, walking along uphill road etc... The performance is humorous, lively and vivid.

Walking on stilts: When performing the dance, the dancer's feet are attached to two stilts about one meter in height. Walking on stilts is usually based on a certain plot, either classical or folk. But sometimes walking on stilts is played only for the sake of the display of the unique skills in the performance.

Temple Fair in the Central-China Plains:

Mt. Song district is also famous for its night temple fair——Jiulongtan (Pond of Nine Dragons) Temple Fair. The Dragon God/Goddess worshiped by the local people is the Queen Mother of Dragon and Dragon King. Legend has it that in the reign of Empress Wu Zetian, a country woman, named Kang Fengying, gave birth to nine dragons and is thence granted the title of Queen Mother of Dragons.

Jiulongtan Temple Fair held on the 15th day in the fifth lunar month is quite influential all over Zhengzhou area. People would go uphill to worship them in the temple on the 14th day in the fifth lunar month. In the evening on the 14th day, pilgrims would pour into Dragon King Temple, burning incense before Buddha and reciting and chanting Buddhist sutras. The most attractive scene is the Henan opera performance near the Hall of Queen Mother of Dragons. Audience may even dance to the rhythm of the opera, pushing the temple fair to its climax.

The Temple Fair is the most distinctive one of the area. It is the celebration of the bumper harvest of wheat; it is the opportunity of prayer for abundant rainfall to ensure a good harvest in autumn; it is the opportunity of prayer for a peaceful and happy life; it is also a good opportunity of the young lovers' amorism.

Odes of Zheng

Odes of Zheng contains folk songs produced by the local people in the State of Zheng. Among 21 odes in it, 15 are love songs. Two thousand five hundred years ago, the devotion of native people in the State of Zheng to love is so striking, without any sad melody in "The Peacock Flies to the Southeast" or any weep in silence in "The Miserable Fate of A Woman". They express their love in every aspect of life, even in the political area and social contact, just like pop songs of today.

As is noted in *Book of Rites*, in early spring, young people go picnicking along the riverbank of Zhen and Wei, which becomes a happy land for courting. This reminds us of the customs remaining in present Yunnan and Guizhou Provinces. In spring, the place outside the east gate to the State of Zheng becomes the kingdom of happiness for the young:

> I went out of the east gate,
> Where the girls were in crowds.
> Although there are so many beauties,
> It is not on them that my thoughts rest.
> She is in white silk and grey coiffure,
> She is my joy !
> I went out by the tower on the covering wall,
> Where the girls were like flowers.
> Although they are like flowers,
> It is not them that I'm thinking of.
> She is in white silk and madder-dyed coiffure,
> It is she that makes me happy !

This ode depicts a marvelous painting of folk custom. According to the custom of the State of Zheng, in early spring, young people can go picnicking and date the ones they love. A young man may make his way in the crowd of girls, finding "his joy".

Odes of Zheng is popular not only among the people, but among officials. In 526 B.C., ambassador of the State of Jin, Han Xuanzi was sent on a diplomatic mission to the State of Zheng. In spring, six Zheng officials saw him off to the suburban area of the State of Zheng. Han Xuanzi asked them to compose poems so that he could know more about the State of Zheng. Zi Xian composed the following poem:

> On the moor is the creeping grass,
> And how heavily it is loaded with dew!
> There was a beautiful woman,
> Lovely, with clear eyes and fine forehead!
> We met together accidentally,
> And so my desire was satisfied.
> On the moor is the creeping grass,
> Heavily covered with dew!
> There was a beautiful woman,

Lovely, with clear eyes and fine forehead!
We met together accidentally,
And she and I were happy together.

A fine moment and a beautiful scene, young couples fell in love at first sight. The official of the State of Zheng depicted this romantic love story to the ambassador from the State of Jin, turning love in the poem into friendship. Han Xuanzi regarded it as the promise of further development of the diplomatic relationship of the two states.

Judging from what is revealed in *Odes of Zheng*, the people in the State of Zheng were quite open-minded.

《诗经·郑风》中描绘过的溱洧风光   Views of Zhen and Wei described in *Book of Odes · Odes of Zheng*

风中 **禅** 动少林

SHAOLIN:
DANCING
IN THE WIND

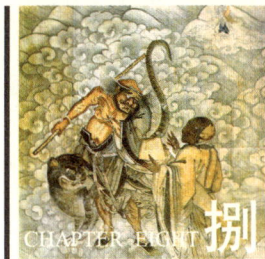

CHAPTER EIGHT 捌

黑色的幽灵窒息了缤纷的烂漫。

鬼眼独觊觎中原，掳掠美丽。天元的反抗是微弱的叹息，素水的屈从是痛苦的悲泣。

花屋破了，在扑面的风雨中，化作满台飘零的落英。

山河碎了，在强寇的铁蹄下，发出仰天的悲鸣。

素水走了，在黑色的狂潮里，留下无限的哀愁。

天元疯了，在欲绝的屈辱中，带着无奈和伤心……

—— 相 关 链 接

禅——人类智慧的一颗明珠

"禅"是梵文的音译，本作"禅那"，简称为"禅"，其意为定，静虑，思维修。但禅宗之"禅"并不限于禅定。它是佛教发展史上一次重大变革，佛教大约在公元前后传入中国，后与中国本土文化相互融合，并随着大批知识精英加入佛学的研究与传播，使佛教中的精华部分——禅宗，被中国的社会伦理思想和思维方式改铸成了独具中国特色的中华禅宗。

禅宗以"不立文字，教外别传，直指人心，见性成佛"，代表着其成熟期的思想。它的根本任务就是在现实生命中动态地把握住超越的佛心、佛性和内在的本心、本性的终极合一。也就是讲，

飞旋、跳跃、呐喊、狂舞……

訇然倒地，世界复归宁静……

    一息尚存的天元下意识地向少林走去，或许，他想起了慧山慈悲的容颜，是否他已听到了佛祖从天界传来的声音？

    当小沙弥奋力拖动天元的造型慢慢隐去，人们看到一缕无处栖息的魂魄，找到了一扇打开的门，一条引渡众生的路径。

    路的尽头可以看见达摩的背影，一千五百多年前的南北朝，一个战乱不止、动荡不安的年代，他怀着一颗慈悲心、智慧心，一苇渡江而来，在中岳嵩山五乳峰上的天然石洞里，默然而坐，九年光阴，破石入影，用自己的身心打造了一艘普度众生的慈航。

    现在天元开始踏上了佛的渡航，在这艘

达摩像 Picture of Dharma

    禅法是使参禅者在当下能够见到自身佛性，发现自身活生生的生命存在。这也正是自唐宋以来中国的文人、士大夫们喜爱参禅的重要原因。

    由于禅宗在参禅方法上，能够将佛教深玄的理论体现在最平凡的日常生活之中，不重冗长的说教，只重实际的证悟，不拘刻板的形式，只重活泼自由，比起其他宗派显得更为平易近人，更为注重实际，更易被追求平易的中国人所接受，所以自唐代以后，中国的宗教、哲学、思想、文化艺术以至人们的日常生活都受到了禅宗的影响。

    在中国禅宗盛极于唐宋两代的同时，其影响已超越了国界。当时朝鲜、日本都不断派僧人来留学求法。禅之悟性，也使东西

灵魂的航船上，负载着我们太多的梦想。俗世的爱恨情仇使

它走得很慢很慢……

少林高僧福裕大师像
Picture of Fu Yu, Ch'an Master in
Shaolin Buddhist Monastery

方思想在更深层的心智领域中交融。今天的西方，禅已蔚为显学，
渗透到西方的哲学、宗教、艺术、医学、心理学、管理学等各个
领域。对于今天的西方人来说，禅已不是仅仅被当做一种新奇的
东方舶来品引进，而是要以西方的思想习惯和语言对禅进行改铸，
使禅成为西方人自己的心灵创作和表现。

A black ghost is stifling the colorful romance.

"One-eye ghost" is invading the Central-China Plains and capturing beautiful women. Tian Yuan is fighting, but his fighting is turning to be a feeble sigh. Su Shui is being taken away, weeping bitterly.

The room full of flowers is collapsing, in the storm and violent wind, turning into fallen petals to cover the ground.

The beautiful land is broken into pieces, sending out miserable shouts under the heels of the valiant bandits.

Su Shui is taken away, leaving endless sorrows and sadness in the dark and violent waves.

Tian Yuan is becoming crazy with broken-hearted mortification, sad and helpless.

He is turning, jumping, crying, dancing crazily...

Suddenly, he is falling down, the world is returning to peace.

Tian Yuan with the last gasp is going to Shaolin subconsciously, perhaps he is thinking of the benevolent look of Master Hui Shan or is hearing Buddha's sound from the sky.

Related Links

Ch'an Buddhism—A Pearl of Human Wisdom

"Ch'an", the transliteration of Sanskrit "dhyana", is originally called "Chan'na", later simplified as "Ch'an". Ch'an not only means "deep meditation" but also "calmness" and "cultivation". As an important change in the history of Buddhism, Buddhism was introduced into China around the beginning of the Christian era, and merged with native Chinese culture gradually. With many intellectuals engaged in the study and dissemination, Ch'an Buddhism, the cream of Buddhism, merged with Chinese ethic and thinking manner, was transformed into Chinese-characteristic Ch'an Buddhism.

The teaching of Ch'an Buddhism in its maturity contains "not setting up of words and letters, not teaching the people who are not Ch'an practitioners, mind-to-mind transmission in a simple, direct manner and to the point, attaining

When the scene of a Buddhist novice dragging strenu-
ously Tian Yuan's body is disappearing gradually, we can
see a wandering soul, finding an open door, a road of Buddhism to deliver all living creatures from torment.

At the end of the road, we can see the figure of Dharma.
In Northern and Southern Dynasties (420 A.D.-589 A.D.) of
more than 1,500 years ago, a turbulent time of wars, he came
here with his benevolence and wisdom, sailing across a river
on a leaf of reed. He entered the cave beneath the Wuru
peak and sat before the cave wall for nine years. When the
feat of cultivation, accomplished by facing the wall, was
completed, his image incredibly appeared on the wall, hence
the famous "wall-facing rock" which can still be seen today.
He uses his image to guide all living creatures to perform
meditation and to be liberated from torment.

Now Tian Yuan is beginning aboard the boat sailing towards Buddha which carries many dreams of us. The earthly
love and hatred have made the boat go slowly.

Buddhahood". The aim of Ch'an is to grasp the ultimate unity of all beings' nature
and mind with the nature and mind of a Buddha. That is, if one can refrain from
thinking of anything and keep our mind blank and free from conceptual thought, he
will see the spontaneous manifestation of essence of the self-mind by itself at that
instant. That is why men of letters and literati since the Tang or the Song Dynasty
have been fond of practicing Ch'an.

Ch'an Buddhism embodies the mystic theory of Buddhism in people's ordinary life, emphasizing actual comprehension instead of wordy and lengthy
preaching, using an active and free way of teaching rather than a mechanical and
dull way. Thus, compared with other sects of Buddhism, Ch'an is more practical
and easier to approach and therefore more easily accepted by amiable Chinese
people. Since the Tang Dynasty, Chinese religion, philosophy, thought, culture, art

and even ordinary life have been influenced by Ch'an Buddhism. Taking literature and philosophy for example, the works of many famous Chinese men of letters, including Tao Yuanming, Wang Wei, Bai Juyi, Wang Anshi and Su Shi, show the influence of Ch'an Buddhism directly, and some scholars studying the history of Chinese ancient philosophy hold that the philosophy history from the Western and Eastern Jin Dynasties, through the Southern and Northern Dynasties, the Sui and the Tang Dynasties, to the period of the Five Dynasties is actually the history of the development of Buddhism in China in which Ch'an is the essence. The Confucian school of idealist philosophy of the Song and the Ming Dynasties was also created under the influence of Garland School (Huayan) and Ch'an, two sects of Buddhism.

Nowadays, while interpreting Ch'an Buddhism, the western world has tried to make use of the teaching of Ch'an Buddhism to rectify the moral degeneration and thoughts in the West. A lot of books and institutes on Ch'an and the centres of Ch'an meditation have appeared like mushrooms after rain, and Ch'an Buddhism has permeated in many fields of philosophy, religion, art, medicine, psychology, management, etc. in the West. For the westerners today, Ch'an has not only been regarded as the novel imported idea from the East, but also transformed Ch'an Buddhism with their own custom and language so as to make Ch'an merge into their creation and manifestation.

风中 SHAOLIN: DANCING IN THE WIND 动少林

CHAPTER NINE 玖

第三幕拉开时,最撩人眼帘的是那满台的红叶和英气风发的武僧挥舞的扫把。扫去的是花屋破碎时洒落的缤纷,还是俗世纷扰的尘埃?这很容易让人想起"风动、幡动还是心动"的故事,以及"本来无一物,何处惹尘埃"的偈语。

当今少林寺高僧释延王禅师写过一首名为《少林传奇》的歌词,是汪美琪演唱的。其中写道:

少林寺的石头哟里面坐着一个人哟,

少林寺的和尚哟心里坐着一个佛哟,

相 关 链 接

少林功夫

少林永信大师认为,少林功夫是在嵩山这一特殊的佛教文化空间中历史地形成的。少林功夫作为庞大的武术体系,在中国武术流派中历史悠久、门类最多、体系最大。据少林寺拳谱记载,少林功夫套路总共约有708套,其中拳术和器械套路552套,另有七十二绝技、擒拿、格斗、卸骨、点穴、气功等各类功法156套。现据少林寺内流传下来和重新收集的少林功夫套路统计,有拳术178套,器械193套,对练59套,其他115套,合计545套。

少林寺的井水哟酸甜苦辣四种味哟，

少林寺的小沙弥敲着一只小木鱼。

少林寺的祖师哟手里提着一只鞋哟，

少林寺的大殿哟地上踩了几道坑哟，

少林寺的罗汉哟春夏秋冬七种色哟，

少林寺的小武僧每天练着真功夫……

　　少林功夫最原始的基本功能是守护寺产，但经过千百年的历史演进、体系完善和境界提升，少林功夫已转变为以文化传承功能为核心，实用功夫与文化功能并举，这是由少林功夫独特的历史地位和本质属性所决定的。

　　1. 从护法到弘法。少林功夫是少林寺和少林禅宗传承体系的识别标志，是少林寺独创的、最有效的弘法手段和接引众生、利乐有情的法门。用现代术语说，少林功夫可以被看成是少林寺和佛教禅宗最具竞争力和沟通力，也是最成功的品牌传播策略和形象识别战略。少林功夫历千年王朝更迭而生生不息，将少林寺、佛教禅宗乃至中华传统文化传遍全球就是实证。少林功夫的功能也因此成功地从护法转向弘法。

与这首歌的情趣异曲同工,《风中少林》里武僧们扫把、板凳一出手,精妙神功处处有;小和尚的随意嬉戏,童趣中也透出无限禅机……

的确,少林功夫信仰的最初形态是禅定。禅宗充满东方智慧对人生的洞彻,使佛教原有的面对死亡悲苦之面貌,变为对人间生之欢乐的肯定。禅宗讲究在现实的日常生活中修行,少林功夫作为少林寺僧人日常生活的组成部分,也被纳入学佛修禅的形式中。

禅,赋予了少林功夫更为丰富的内容。少林功夫带给禅者特有的轻松、自在、神化之境界。

　　2. 文化传承功能。修习少林功夫,是身心合一地体验中国传统文化的方便门径。从其内容构成看,少林功夫是技术体系,也是传统文化宝库。首先,少林功夫是以套路为基本单位,每个套路又由多则上百个、少则几十个的动作组合而成。动作之间的连接设计,不仅严格遵循人体运动规律以及对手的反应,同时也充分融入了中国传统哲学思想精华(如阴阳平衡、刚柔相济、天人合一等),体现了儒释道三教合一的禅宗精神。其次,套路与套路之间,不是孤立存在的,而是相互之间有所照应。表面上看,它是按照难易次第排列,是学习的阶梯或模式;深入地看,实为中国古代思维方式之表现,是中国传统文化的特殊模式。

　　痛苦中的天元无意修禅，他的胸中只是思念，思念远方被掳掠的妻子；只是羞辱，一个男人无奈的仇恨。痛苦煎熬中的天元神情恍惚，思念、羞辱、仇恨交织的网不得解脱。

　　从某种意义上来说，天元回到少林，是因为少林功夫。少林寺的耳濡目染，使他知道少林功夫的神奇无比。仇恨是跳出刀鞘的利剑，习武是复仇的权杖。

　　他向慧山跪下男儿的铁膝。

　　3. 激励个体自我实现。修禅习武互相促进，有助于达成人生最高境界。因为少林功夫是一个技术知识体系，其中隐含着一套严格的学习模式，所以很自然地被少林寺僧人转化为学佛修禅的程序。在少林功夫成为僧人学佛修禅的手段以后，僧人们又会反过来将佛教无常无我的生活方式、道德戒律和对大智大勇精神的追求，注入少林功夫，使少林功夫的内涵和品质得以提升，达到"禅武合一"的境界。这就是古人所说的"禅武不二法门"。

　　4. 自成体系的养生健身功能。少林功夫讲究动静结合、阴阳平衡、刚柔相济、神形兼备，其中最著名的是"六合"理论：手与足合、肘与膝合、肩与胯合、心与意合、意与气合、气与力合。

　　慧山给天元的不是剑而是扫把，拂去内心的尘埃，掠走性情的浮躁。芸芸众生，见性成佛。见性即是将心放下而不执著于放下，见色即空而又不沉迷于空，发超度世人之愿而不记功德，遁入空门而远离尘世。

　　扫把之舞可以说是舞武结合的绝妙一笔，少林拳枪刀棍之术融为行云流水的舞蹈，实在是来自深居三皇寨，禅、武、医集于一身的德建大师的点化，舞蹈编导晓荷、张弋夫妇和香港"元家班"其貌不扬的元晖的得意之举。

　　"年轮"一段是《风中少林》令人过目不忘的华彩：

　　银光闪闪的九节鞭舞出春天嫩绿的生机，

　　虎虎生风的双截棍舞出夏天清新的活力，

　　威风八面的少林枪舞出秋天绚丽的风采，

　　出神入化的少林刀舞出冬天素洁的诗意……

　　塔林伴着星辰日月飞快地游移，

　　少林武僧飞檐走壁的身影间，四季在眼前美妙地轮回……

　　"天人合一"的思想认为，最合乎人体自然结构的动作，才是最合理的。去芜存菁留传下来的少林功夫套路，都是非常珍贵的精华，能使人体潜能高度发挥，加上博大精深的少林医宗体系，用于养生健身，功效可靠而且十分强劲。

　　5. 少林功夫将人体潜能发挥到极限时，同时也展现了人类形体美学的至高境界。它是中国古代人体运动美学的精华所在，它含蓄内刚，坚实有力，"静如处子，动如脱兔"，笼罩在静穆的佛教文化氛围中，具有震撼人心的独特审美价值。少林功夫套路现尚存545套之多，即有545种组合变化，美不胜收，是人体运动艺术的宝库。

"天下功夫出少林"，少林功夫从达摩自创的《易筋经》走来，一路上继承、吸收、创新，拥有了内容丰富、套路繁多的内外功夫。

它博法百家，荟萃天下。它式出原典，武行文意。

它积习仿生，俗雅兼具。它禅修武医，拳贯中西……

它内静外猛，朴实无华，变化无穷，技法精湛。

它声东击西，指上打下，虚虚实实，刚柔相济。

它随缘而化，随心而动，随神而往，随行而发。

它无招可依，无法可循，一切如行云流水，天人合一。

在这里，我们看不到武术逼人的杀机，看到的只有时光的流逝。

在这里，世俗的风尘纷纷飘落，留下的，是物我两忘的惬意。

这就是武术禅——禅心运武，透彻人生。一招一式凝结着历代高僧大师和儒士大夫所构成的精英群体对宇宙奥秘、人生真谛的体验和悟解。

6. 少林功夫长期以来作为民族精神的象征，具有自立、自强、信义、正气的社会导向。少林功夫的精神品格与少林寺历史密切相关。有着1500多年历史的少林寺，作为佛教禅宗祖庭和中华武术圣地，从清初（17世纪）开始，即被赋予民族政治寓意，少林功夫成为中华民族精神力量的重要象征。

少林《易筋经》中的练功图　Drawings of Shaolin Monks Practicing Kung Fu Described in *Yijinjing*

一拳一脚练就不动心意，走向禅武合一的佳境……

天元的净发剃度，我们还不知道是否也割断了尘世的情缘，但我们依然可以感到他激烈悲切的胸怀。

Shaolin Martial Monks Practicing Kung Fu in Snow　在雪中修炼的少林武僧

禅武同源

高僧释延王在文章中写道：少林功夫本质是禅武，一是禅与武本为一体，二是禅为武的定语，即"禅之武"。少林功夫以禅为理论基础，而禅是佛的修证法门。佛法无边，禅法无穷。

禅与武为何"本为一体"？首先是禅武同源。一是源于少林，即禅与武同时起源于中岳嵩山五乳峰前的少林寺。所以少林寺是中国佛教禅宗祖庭，同时也是少林功夫发祥地。禅与武在这里同时诞生，自然有它的契机，这契机就在于禅与武的共性。

佛教起源于古印度，传入中国后与中国传统文化、民族文化和民俗民风相结合，渐渐汉化成"中国佛教"。中国佛教有八大宗，禅宗是最具中国特色的佛教宗派。佛教的东传和禅宗的创立，给中国文化带来了新的血液，于是有了禅诗、禅画、禅茶、禅曲，乃至雕刻、建筑等也都展现出禅的魅力。中国武术早已有之，最初是以角斗和养生为主，多表现在侠士、隐士和军人身上。当中国传统武技与中国禅宗相结合时，一个新的武术流派——少林功夫自然就诞生了。

二是源于生活。佛教说行、住、坐、卧皆是修行，禅宗说吃饭、穿衣、睡觉皆是禅。少林功夫以禅入武，由武入禅，打拳习武自古为少林寺僧人的日常生活，为每天的必修课，就像吃饭、穿衣、睡觉一样平常而重要。习武本身就是少林僧人修禅的法门。同时，少林僧人和少林弟子们在修禅习武的同时，从生活中得到感悟，向生活学习，创编功法与招式，不断完善、充实少林功夫。如达摩祖师面壁之时，常走出洞外活动筋骨，伸伸懒腰，这就是少林《易筋经》中"双手托天势"的来源，紧那罗王每天烧火做饭而悟出"少林烧火棍"，还有绳鞭、草镰、铁勺、禅杖等既为劳动和生活工具，又为少林武僧常用兵器。

三是源于自然。禅是大智慧，是通达智慧彼岸的桥梁，是了悟宇宙人生真谛的法门，是人与自然的沟通。佛说一切众生皆有佛性。五禽六畜、虫鱼鸟兽乃至花草树木等世间万物都是宇宙生命的组成部分，有一个共性，这个共性就是佛性。人类来于自然，归于自然，世间万法皆如此。少林僧人和少林弟子们在修禅习武之余，观察自然，在自然界中寻发展。如模仿动物的形体动作及功能特性，创作出大批优秀、经典的功法与套路，如少林五形拳等，皆是人对自然的感悟。

四是源于自心。禅的最大特点就是一个悟字。如何悟？从自心去悟。达摩祖师面壁九年，而悟中国禅宗。二祖慧可断臂求法，而悟达摩精髓。六祖慧能大师闻《金刚经》"应无所住，而生其心"，开创禅宗"顿悟法门"。以禅入武的少林功夫，自然也讲究悟。从这方面讲，少林功夫分体能和智能两个层次。习武人只要吃苦，就能长功。当练到一定火候，光是吃苦就不行了，得靠悟性。悟性好，就能更上一层楼，进入新的境界。这也就是武术与武学、武道的关系所在。武术能治人，武学、武道能治国治军，也就是人生之大道。所以说，练少林功夫，能修禅悟禅，是少林寺所独有的修佛法门。

少林寺白衣殿的练武壁画
Mural Paintings of Shaolin Monks Practicing Kung Fu in the White Robe Hall of Shaolin Buddhist Monastery

When Act Three begins, the most spectacular scene is the red leaves covering the stage and the broom being waved by a handsome and vigorous martial monk. What is he sweeping away, the broken pieces of the flower room or the dust disturbing the earthly people? Also it is reminding us of the story of "What is moving, the wind, the streamer, or your heart?" and a verse of Buddhism which says: "there is nothing in you except the will, how could you be troubled with a speck of dust?"

Ch'an master Shi Yan-wang, contemporary monk-saint of Shaolin Buddhist Monastery, wrote the lyrics for a song entitled "Legend of Shaolin" which was sung by a singer Wang Meiqi. It reads as follows:

In a stone cave of Shaolin Buddhist Monastery sits a man;

In the heart of every monk of Shaolin Buddhist Monastery lives a Buddha;

In Shaolin Buddhist Monastery the well water has got four flavors: sour, sweet, bitter and hot;

A young sramanera is knocking at a small wooden fish.

Related Links

Shaolin Kung Fu

Shaolin Kung Fu, originated in Shaolin Buddhist Monastery, is well-known all over the world for its long history, deep and extensive Buddhist culture, unique way of going down to later generations and integrated system. It has been developed gradually in Shaolin Buddhist Monastery at Mt. Song where Buddhist culture has been developed well.

As a colossal martial system, Shaolin Kung Fu has been the sect with the longest history, the largest number of branches and the biggest system among all the Wushu sects in China. Meanwhile, it is a sect that surpasses all the other sects. According to *Collection of Shaolin Boxing Skills*, altogether there are originally 708 routines of serial skills. As one of the largest and earliest schools, Shaolin Kung Fu consists of 552 fist and weapon routines as well as 156 routines of other

The Patriarch of Shaolin Buddhist Monastery is holding a shoe,

Some footprints are left in the Mahavira Hall ,

The arhats of Shaolin Buddhist Monastery spend their spring, summer, autumn and winter there,

The young martial monks practice Kung Fu everyday...

Shaolin in the Wind displays the same scenery in the song: martial monks are showing their consummate Kung Fu with just brooms and benches; the young monks' casual sport also displays the theory of Ch'an Buddhism.

Indeed, the initial belief of Shaolin Kung Fu is Ch'an meditation. Being full of the perception of life made by the Oriental men of wisdom, Ch'an Buddhism has turned the original teaching of Buddhism, in which life contains sufferings to face death and sorrow, into the affirmation of earthly happiness. As Ch'an Buddhism holds that people can cultivate themselves in ordinary life, the practice of Shaolin martial art has become a part of ordinary life of Shaolin monks and can therefore be regarded as one way of Ch'an Meditation.

Ch'an helps enrich the connotation of Shaolin Kung Fu while Shaolin Kung Fu brings Ch'an practitioners a more

techniques such as 72-arts, snatching, parrying, wrestling, bone-breaking and hard and soft Qigong exercises. According to the present statistics, there are altogether 545 routines of martial art which have been handed down and collected again in Shaolin Buddhist Monastery, including 178 routines of boxing, 193 routines of weapon skills, 59 routines of defending and exercising skills and 115 routines of other skills.

The initial function of Shaolin Kung Fu was to protect the properties of the temple. However, after thousands of years' development and perfection, Shaolin Kung Fu has combined its function of spreading and inheriting the culture with its practical function. This is decided by its unique historical position and nature.

1. Preserving and Developing Buddhism.

Shaolin Kung Fu is the symbol of Shaolin Buddhist Monastery and Shaolin

relaxed, freer and better state of mind.

Miserable Tian Yuan finds it hard to focus his attention on Ch'an meditation, because of his missing to his wife, who is carried far away from him by the brutal bandits. Unable to get out of the net woven with humiliation, hatred and longing, Tian Yuan is becoming more miserable and more troubled.

To some degree, it is Shaolin Kung Fu that makes Tian Yuan go to Shaolin Buddhist Monastery. Knowing that Shaolin Kung Fu was powerful and miraculous, he decides to practice Kung Fu to make revenge.

He is throwing himself at Master Hui Shan's feet.

However, Master Hui Shan gives Tian Yuan a broom rather than a sword. He wants him to sweep away the dust in his heart and get rid of the impulsive nature. All living beings putting away all their cares will attain Buddhahood through meditation.

The broom dance in *Shaolin in the Wind* may be regarded as the perfect union of dance and Wushu. The idea of merging Shaolin boxing skills, spear skills, falchion skills, sword skills and stick skills into the dance comes

Ch'an Buddhism, invented by Shaolin Buddhist Monastery and an effective way of spreading the beliefs and the initial approach which leads all beings to become a Buddhist believer. Having survived for thousands of years, Shaolin Kung Fu has spread the fame of Shaolin Buddhist Monastery, Ch'an Buddhism and traditional Chinese culture over the world.

2. Inheriting and spreading culture

Practicing Shaolin Kung Fu is an easier way of experiencing traditional Chinese culture with both one's body and mind. From the respect of content, Shaolin Kung Fu is not only a huge technical system, but also an important treasure-house of traditional Chinese culture. Firstly, Shaolin Kung Fu takes a series of actions as its basic unit which consist of dozens or even hundreds of actions played in succession. The design of connecting one action with another not only follows

from Yuan Hui, plain-looking but greatly talented, a member of the famous "Yuan Family" for martial art training in Hong Kong.

"Annual Ring" is one splendid scene in *Shaolin in the Wind*:

The sparkling Shaolin nine-node-scourge is played in springs full of greenness and vitality,

The two-node-stick is waved vigorously in summers full of fragrance and vigor,

Shaolin spear is pricked impressively in beautiful autumns,

Shaolin falchion is brandished mystically in white winters.

The Pagoda Forest is moving with the accompaniment of the sun, the moon and the stars;

Shaolin martial monks are flying and leaping from one roof to another, four seasons of a year are taking turns alternatively...

It is well known that "All types of Kung Fu have originated from Shaolin Buddhist Monastery". Since *Yijinjing* was created by Bodhidharma, through a process of inheriting,

strictly the motion rules of the body and the response of the opponent but is also mixed sufficiently with the cream of traditional Chinese philosophy such as "*Yin-yang* balance", "coupling hardness with softness" and "unity of man and heaven", which embodies Ch'an spirit, the combination of Confucianism, Buddhism and Taoism. Secondly, series of actions do not exist side by side but coincide with each other.

Superficially, series of actions are performed according to the mode of learning from the easier to the more difficult. But in fact, it is the representation of ancient Chinese thinking style and traditional Chinese culture.

3. Motivating an individual to make self-realization

Ch'an meditation and practicing Kung Fu can be promoted with each other and be helpful for a man to reach the consummate state of life. Because Shaolin absorbing and innovating, Shaolin Kung Fu now possesses internal and external Kung Fu of rich connotation and include many routines of serial skills.

It learns from all the other Wushu schools and has become one of the best school of martial art in the world.

It imitates the movements of animals and becomes popular among both ordinary and cultured people.

It seems violent on the surface, but turns out to be gentle, plain and changeable, replete with consummate skills.

It makes a feint to fight in one way while attacks in another, aims at the upper and attacks the lower, and combines softness with hardness.

It adapts itself to different circumstances, and manifests great flexibility with one's lot, mind, spirit as well as movement.

It does not follow the definite rules and goes naturally and smoothly, reaching a state of the unity of heaven and human.

In here, you can only see the passage of the time rather than the murderous look of ordinary Wushu. In here, all earthly cares go away, and what is left is the satisfaction of

Kung Fu is a technical system which contains a strict mode of learning, it is naturally accepted as the standard way of learning Buddhism and Ch'an meditation by the monks of Shaolin Buddhist Monastery. On the other hand, by infusing the natural living style of Buddhists, moral and religious principles and the spirit of pursuing wisdom and bravery into Shaolin Kung Fu, the monks of Shaolin Buddhist Monastery have promoted the connotation and quality of Shaolin Kung Fu and made it reach the state of "unity of Ch'an and Wushu". That is what ancient people said "the only way to reach Ch'an and Wushu".

4. Preserving one's health and building up one's body

The actions and series of actions of Shaolin Kung Fu stress the principles such as the combination of motion and stillness, *Yin-yang* balance, coupling hardness with softness, and embracing shape and spirit. Among them there is a fa-the audience who forget all the things around them.

That is the unique Shaolin martial art, combined with Ch'an Buddhism, practiced to help people to comprehend life. Every action of Shaolin Kung Fu shows the experience and comprehension of Ch'an masters and literati of past dynasties on the mystic universe and life.

By repeating the practice of Wushu skills and meditating, a man reaches the consummate state of the unity of Ch'an and Wushu.

Though Tian Yuan takes the tonsure and becomes a monk, we don't know whether he has forgotten his earthly love and we can still feel his sadness and anger.

mous theory of "six unities": unity of hands and feet, unity of elbows and knees, unity of shoulders and hips, unity of heart and mind, unity of mind and *Qi* and unity of *Qi* and strength. The idea of "unity of man and heaven" holds that the natural action that best suits the human body is the most reasonable. After a long time's test, discarding the dross and selecting the essential, the series of actions of Shaolin Kung Fu handed down from ancient times are a valuable essence and can develop the human potential fully. Combined with broad and profound Shaolin Ch'an medical system, it is reliable and efficient in preserving one's health and building one's body. *Yijinjing* and *Xisuijing*, two well-known books which combine the Ch'an medicine and Ch'an Wushu, deal with the good way to build up a good physique and improve man's health.

5. Shaolin Kung Fu can give full play to the potential of human body as well

as display the consummate state of physical aesthetics. The traditional Shaolin Kung Fu, after 1,500 years' invention and refinement by generations of Shaolin monks, has been the gem of the traditional Chinese culture and the essence of ancient Chinese motion aesthetics of human body. Reserved and indomitable, firm and forceful, when it is performed, it is as static as a virgin and as dynamic as a running rabbit. Immersed in the solemn Buddhist culture, Shaolin Kung Fu owns the unique and shaking value. As 545 series of actions exist in Shaolin Kung Fu now, that is, 545 series of combinations and changes of arms and legs, it is really the art treasure of human motion.

6. As the symbol of our national spirit for a long time, Shaolin Kung Fu can lead people to self-reliance, honesty and justice. Such quality of Shaolin Kung Fu is intimately related to the history of Shaolin Buddhist Monastery. Shaolin Buddhist Monastery with a history of more than 1,500 years has always been the ancestral court of Ch'an Buddhism and the sacred place of Chinese Wushu. Since the beginning of Qing Dynasty (17 century A.D.), it has been embodied with the connotation of politics and become the symbol of the spirit of the Chinese nation.

Notes:

Shaolin Wushu (Shaolin Martial Art) is one of the most influential genres of Chinese martial art, and it's named after the Shaolin Buddhist Monastery located in Dengfeng County, Henan Province. The monks in the Shaolin Buddhist Monastery began to study martial art during the Southern and Northern Dynasties and this tradition prevailed during the Sui and the Tang dynasties (581-907).

Shaolin Wushu is famous both at home and abroad as a highly effective method of self-defense and health-building. Combining both external and internal, and "hard" and "soft" exercises, Shaolin Wushu involves various methods of fighting techniques, consisting of barehanded boxing and weaponry combat. The Shaolin boxing has compactly designed routines. Its movements are quick, powerful and flexible; both practical for defense and attack.

The most outstanding characteristic of Shaolin boxing is that the practitioner works on one straight line. It means that his movements of advancing, retreating, turning around, sideways, or jumping are restrained on one line. His arms are kept slightly bent so that he can stretch out to attack or withdraw freely for self defense. Another characteristic of Shaolin Wushu is to maintain the body in perfect balance, as stable as a mountain. The practitioners should keep a tranquil mind but strike with great force and speed. He should be good at "borrowing" force from the opponent. That is, he should not meet the opponent's strikes head-on, but take advantage of the striker's force and go along with it to bring him to ward off a force of a thousand weights. The practitioner should know how to make feigned strikes and when striking, hit the vital parts of the opponent. The movements should be as dextrous as a cat's, the shaking as a tiger's, the moving as a dragon's, the advancing as lightning and the yelling as thunder.

Shaolin Wushu is a very convenient sport, for the practice does not need a large space and is not affected by weather or the kind of weapons used.

There are many routines. External exercises include Minor Hong Boxing, Greater Hong Boxing, Old Hong Boxing, Chaoyang Boxing, Chang Boxing, Plum Blossom Boxing, Cannon Boxing, Luohan Buddha Boxing, Tongbei Boxing, Seven-star Boxing, Dragon-out-of-the-sea Boxing and Shooting-star Boxing; for internal exercises there are Xingyi Boxing and Juji Boxing. Shaolin boxing can be practiced singly or in pairs. The dual routines include: Banshou Liuhe Boxing, Yaoshou Liuhe Boxing and Kick and Strike Liuhe Boxing.

The Same Root of Ch'an and Kung Fu

The nature of Shaolin Kung Fu is Ch'an martial art for two reasons: one is that Ch'an Buddhism and martial art originally belong to one unity, and the other is that Ch'an is the modifier of martial art, ie. the martial art of Ch'an. It is based on the theory of Ch'an which is the initial approach to becoming a Buddhist believer. With all-powerful Buddhist sutras and Ch'an theory as its foundation, Shaolin Kung Fu has naturally become well-known all over the world.

The same root of Ch'an Buddhism and martial art indicates two things. Firstly, it is because they have the same origin. Both of them originated from Shaolin Buddhist Monastery which is located in front of Wuru Peak of Mt. Song. Shaolin Buddhist Monastery has been regarded as the ancestral court of Ch'an Buddhism in China and the birthplace of Shaolin Kung Fu. The reason why both Ch'an Buddhism and Kung Fu were born in the same place at the same time is the destiny which lies in the homogeneity of them.

Originated in ancient India, Buddhism has been combined with traditional Chinese culture and customs and assimilated as Chinese Buddhism since its introduction into China. There are eight sects of Buddhism in which Ch'an sect has the most distinctive Chinese characteristics. The introduction of Buddhism into the East and the creation of Ch'an Buddhism have infused fresh blood into Chinese culture and made it reach its height of power and splendors for several times. The glamour of Ch'an Buddhism could also be found in Ch'an poems, Ch'an paintings, Ch'an tea theory, Ch'an music, and even in scripture and architecture.

Chinese Wushu has existed since ancient times. At the earliest stage, it was mainly used for boxing and preserving health, practiced by expert swordsmen, hermits and soldiers. When traditional Chinese Wushu combined with Ch'an Buddhism, a new martial art sect, Shaolin Kung Fu was born.

Secondly, both Ch'an Buddhism and martial art originated from ordinary life. Buddhism holds that all human actions including walking, standing, sitting and sleeping are forms of practicing Buddhism while Ch'an declares that eating, dressing and sleeping are forms of practicing Ch'an meditation. Shaolin Kung Fu infuses Ch'an meditation into martial art and martial art into Ch'an meditation. Practicing martial art, like eating, dressing and sleeping, is an important part of Shaolin martial monks' ordinary life and daily task. Practicing martial art itself is the initial approach to attaining Buddhahood for Shaolin monks. While practicing martial art with Ch'an meditation, Shaolin monks and disciples have made innovations consistently on skills of martial art and improved Shaolin Kung Fu through their learning and experiencing life. While the Buddhist master Dharma was facing the wall,

少林寺迎宾雕塑
Statue of Welcome at Shaolin Buddhist Monastery

he usually went out of the cave to straighten his back and exercise his body. That's the origin of the action "Two hands stretching out to the sky" in *Yijinjing* of Shaolin Buddhist Monastery. King Jinnaluo worked out the routines of skills named "Shaolin Fire Cudgel" based on his daily work of tendinging fire and cooking meals. The weapons used by Shaolin martial monks such as whips, sickles, iron ladles and the Buddhist wand are also used as the tools in laboring and living.

Thirdly, both of them originated from nature. As the great wisdom, Ch'an is the bridge to wisdom, the approach to getting the true meaning of life and universe and the communication of man and nature. Buddhism claims that as the component of the universe, all beings, animals, birds, flowers, trees, etc. own the nature of Buddha. Like all the other things, man comes from nature and returns to nature finally. While practicing Kung Fu and Ch'an meditation, Shaolin monks and disciples have observed nature and developed Kung Fu in nature. By imitating the movements of the beasts and birds, they have created lots of classical series actions, such as Shaolin Five-element Boxing (based on the Chinese traditional philosophy of the Five Elements—Gold, Wood, Water, Fire and Earth).

At last, both of them originated from man's heart. The most important trait of Ch'an is realization. How to achieve it? Use your heart. Facing the wall silently for nine years, the first Patriarch Dharma created the Chinese Ch'an. Cutting one arm to show his determination to attain Buddhism, the second Patriarch Hui-Ke was enlightened with the essence of Dharma. Hearing the theory in *The Truths of Vajra Prajna Paramita Sutr*a, a famous Buddhist sutra, the sixth Patriarch Hui-Neng obtained "the sudden realization of the approach to becoming a Buddhist believer" of Ch'an Buddhism. Converged with Ch'an, Shaolin Kung Fu is also particular about realization. If practicing hard, the skill of Wushu practitioners would be better. Yet at a certain stage, martial skills could be developed only through realization. Good realization can improve martial art skills. That's the relationship of martial art and the theories and doctrines of martial art. Martial art can be used to run a country and direct military affairs. Therefore, practicing Shaolin Kung Fu is the unique way of Shaolin monks to attain Buddhahood.

风中 SHAOLIN: DANCING IN THE WIND 动少林

遥远的塞外，顾影自怜的素水心中盈满了撕心裂肺的苦楚。

强暴蹂躏的伤痛伴着花开花落的等待，长夜难眠的泪眼流出无穷无尽的思念……

素水那催人泪下的独舞，让人想起杜甫思乡的诗。

社会的动乱，皇帝的偏执，朝廷的弄权，官场的倾轧，先后让"诗圣"丢官，逃难，陷贼，漂泊无依，颠沛流离。

相关链接

郑州唐诗三大家

杜甫（712—770年），字子美，生于河南巩县瑶湾（今郑州巩义市南瑶湾村），自称"杜陵布衣"，是中国文学史上伟大的现实主义诗人。杜甫一生写下了一千多首诗，其中著名的有"三吏"、"三别"、《兵车行》《茅屋为秋风所破歌》《丽人行》《春望》等。杜甫的诗是唐帝国由盛转衰的艺术记录。杜甫以积极的入世精神，用诗歌勇敢、

杜甫像　Picture of Du Fu

　　诗人思念他的家乡，曾深情地吟诵："露从今夜白，月是故乡明"，"花落辞故枝，风回返无处"，那种盼归而不得归的惆怅，是化不开的伤感情结。

　　杜甫的乡思，在素水的舞步里倾诉……

忠实、深刻地反映了极为广泛的社会现实。他的诗具有丰富的社会内容、鲜明的时代色彩和强烈的政治倾向，激荡着热爱祖国、热爱人民的炽烈情感和不惜自我牺牲的崇高精神。因此，杜甫被后人尊称为"诗圣"，他的诗也被公认为"诗史"。1962年，杜甫被定为世界文化名人。

Poetic Picture of Du Fu　杜甫诗意画

鬼眼独如黑色的幽灵又在舞台上游走，大军压境。

素水张开纤细的手臂。

是否这就是爱的极致？

在穷凶极恶的强寇面前，为了挽救恋人的生命，素水忍辱投进了魔掌。也正是凭着这种爱，她用自己的牺牲，换来了天元生的希望。

在大厦将倾的时刻，为了家乡的安宁，素水义无反顾地张开了阻挡的臂膀。尽管，她柔弱的身躯，无力挡住践踏的魔爪、汹涌的浊浪！

这就是一个貌似柔弱的中原女子，爱得如此热烈，爱得如此深沉！

白居易像　Image of Bai Juyi

白居易（772—846年），字乐天，晚年号香山居士，生于河南新郑东郭宅（今郑州新郑市东郭寺村）。白居易是杜甫之后唐代又一位杰出的现实主义诗人，也是唐代诗人中作品最多的一个，其《长恨歌》、《琵琶行》等都是中国文化界人人皆知的名篇。他曾将自己的诗分为四类：讽喻、闲适、感伤、杂律。白居易的语言通俗平易，这是与他平易浅切、明畅通俗的诗风紧密相联的。白诗文字浅显，很少用典故和古奥的词句，还特别喜欢提炼民间口语、俗语入诗。但白诗的诗意并不浅显，他常以浅白之句寄托讽喻之意，取得触目惊心的艺术效果。

Poetic Picture of Bai Juyi's "Song of the Pipa Player"　白居易《琵琶行》诗意图

李商隐像　Picture of Li Shangyin

　　李商隐（813—858年），字义山，别号玉谿生，又号樊南生，原籍怀州河内（今河南沁阳），其祖父李甫迁居郑州荥阳，遂为荥阳人。李商隐是晚唐诗坛的一颗明星。他的多愁善感，以及繁博的事象和复杂的意念，在他的诗里往往是避实就虚，透过一种象征手法表现出来。这种象征手法建筑在丰富而美妙的想象的基础上，因而他笔下的意象，有时如七宝流苏那样缤纷绮丽，有时又像流云走月那样活泼空明，给人以强烈的美感。他的近体诗，尤其是七律更有独特的风格，绣织丽字，镶嵌典故，包藏细密，意境朦胧，对诗的艺术形式发展有重大贡献。

然而，当她逃回中原，与皈依佛门的天元再次相遇，无论如何地悲伤缠绵，也终于无法唤回天元那颗已经出世的心。

天元与素水寺院重逢算得上全剧的华彩乐章，这对曾经相濡以沫的夫妻历尽苦难，如今近在咫尺，却似天各一方。天元欲爱不能、欲罢不舍的凄苦无奈，素水撕心裂肺的悲怆，催人泪下。唐建平的音乐天才在这里发挥得淋漓尽致，如泣如诉的旋律似裂帛碎玉，令人潸然泪下。

如果说，《风中少林》的武术，武出的是这片土地的英雄本色，

如果说，《风中少林》的舞蹈，舞出的是这片土地的诗画风情，

如果说，《风中少林》的舞台，再现的是这片土地的厚重底蕴，

佛与爱

"佛"是一种境界，是一种互动性极强的深层次的爱。

这种爱，源于内心，源远流长，植于圣洁，弥漫人间，包容众生！

这种爱，重在施予，勤于播洒，不计得失，不求回报，普度众生！

关于佛抑或是关于爱，无关乎拒绝还是接受——只要佛在心中，爱在心里——就够了。爱并被接受，是两情相悦；爱不被接受，也并非两厢无缘。对"佛"来说，对爱的拒绝，也许是一种更厚重的爱的施予和接纳。

　　那么,《风中少林》的音乐，则画龙点睛地勾描出了这片土地的灵魂。在惊心动魄、充满张力的旋律里，分明听到了河南梆子的大腔大调、黄河号子的浑厚激昂。

　　在余音绕梁、美轮美奂的华彩中，飘荡着郑韩故城战国编钟醇正圆润的清音。

　　还有那熟悉亲切的三弦、唢呐,还有那贴心贴肺的民歌、小调……

　　这一切，无不是这片土地的天籁之声！

　　爱是甜蜜的，更是苦痛的。爱是人类永远的追求，是人生恒定的主题。人，因爱而生，因爱而荣，因爱而痛，因爱而苦，因爱而爱，因爱而恨。

　　爱是有层次的。平凡之爱，是以被接纳为动机的付出，是以给予为前提的收受。而"佛"之爱，也是一种付出，却是一种无私的给予；也是一种接受，却是一种宽容厚重的容纳。

当天元丢下见证夫妻恩爱的丝帕时，我们不知应该去怜悯他还是去谴责他，但对于天元来讲，他似乎完成了他的觉悟。

对觉悟者，

伟大的道路从不艰难。

当爱和恨一同消失，

万物变得清澈透明，

一切呈现本性。

我们看到了最细微的差别，

那就是天空和大地的差别。

郑州民歌

从新石器时期七孔埙的发现和战国编钟发出的大小三度音程，到巩义石窟北魏时期各种乐器的原型，还有汉代画像砖上的乐舞表演、唐代彩绘女舞俑的演出、宋代乐舞伎人的载歌载舞，无不述说着郑州地区音乐艺术源远流长的历史。

遗憾的是，《诗经·郑风》只留下了21首脍炙人口的民歌歌词，至于曲谱，大多湮没在了历史的长河。好在还有口口相传的民歌，自生自灭中延续着远古的旋律。

郑州民歌按照题材和演唱方式的不同，大致可分为号子、山歌、小调、歌舞小调、叙事歌和儿歌等。

Seven-hole *Xun* (an ancient musical instrument) of the New Stone Age Unearthed in Zhengzhou　郑州出土的新石器时期七孔埙

其中反映劳动生产的，主要有黄河"船工号子"、"夯歌"、"板车号子"等。郑州、巩义、荥阳一带的黄河虽水流平缓，但不少拉船的"黄河号子"，如"满号"、"揽船号"、"撤船号子"、"推船号子"、"起锚号子"等，旋律高亢激越、起伏跌宕。新密、新郑、巩义等地，有"过顶夯歌"、"打夯号子"等夯歌，其节奏平直有力、简洁明快、质朴豪放。此外，搬运工人还有鼓劲加油的"板车号子"。号子的演唱形式多是一人领唱、众人合腔。号子的词，除无实意的单纯呼号外，其他往往是即兴创作，风趣乐观，能消除疲劳、统一节奏。其旋律规整，起伏不大，又朗朗上口，便于传唱。

在郑州民歌中，小调较多，曲词比较完整、稳定，旋律温婉优美、悦耳动听，如《十对花》、《放风筝》等，反映了群众的思想感情和生产生活。此外，广泛流传的民歌还有田歌、经歌和儿歌等。

郑州民歌的曲调中，宫、商、角、徵、羽五种调式都有应用，尤以徵、宫两种调式为最多。使用的音阶丰富，大量的民歌使用五声音阶，形成了曲调平稳流畅、柔和优美的风格。

郑州出土的春秋编钟
The Set of Bells(or chimes) of the Spring and Autumn Period Unearthed in Zhengzhou

河南博物院的古乐表演　Ancient Court Music Performance in Henan Museum

Wandering about the north of the Great Wall, lonely Su Shui is filled with bitterness:

In grief, Su Shui cherishes the hope of reunion with Tian Yuan, and keeps awake all night long for her affection to Tian Yuan...

The moving solo dance by Su Shui reminds people of the poems written by Du Fu.

The social upheaval, stubbornly biased emperor, and political corruption made the "poet-sage" suffer a period of hardship. Du Fu felt homesick, and ever wrote the poem: "He knows that the dewdrops tonight will be frost. How much brighter the moonlight is at home!" and "Blown down by wind, faded and fallen flowers could no longer grow on trees". The melancholy in the great poet's homesickness reveals his sentimental complex.

The homesickness of Du Fu is wonderfully annotated in Su Shui's solo dance...

Like a black ghost, the brutal bandit "one-eye ghost" is appearing again on the stage and commanding a large contingent of bandits to approach here.

Su Shui is stretching out her thin arms towards him.

Related Links
Three Greatest Tang Poets in Zhengzhou District

Du Fu (712-770), born in Gongyi, Henan Province, is often considered the greatest of Chinese poets. In his life, he composed more than 1,000 poems, among which the most influential are "Pressgang at Stone Moat Village", "A song of War-chariots", "My Cottage Unroofed by Autumn Gales", "A Song of Fair Women", and "A Spring View". Du Fu's poems are an eyewitness to the historical events in a critical period that saw a great, prosperous nation ruined by military rebellions and wars with bordering tribes. His works reveal his loyalty and love to the country, his aspirations and frustrations, his unbounded sympathy for the sad plight of the common people. Hence he is also called Poet-Historian and the Poet-Sage. He was granted the title of World Cultural Celebrity in 1962.

Is this the supreme love?

Facing the ferocious enemies, Su Shui is flinging herself into the devil's hands in order to save her lover's life and the peace of her homeland, though she is so delicate and power-less to struggle with the devil's clutches and tempestuous foul waves.

This is a girl of the Central-China Plains who is seem-ingly delicate! How ardent and profound her love is!

However, having escaped from the evil hands of "one-eye ghost" and returned to the Central-China Plains, she meets Tian Yuan again who has already been converted to Buddhism. No matter how mournful and sentimental she is, she couldn't change Tian Yuan's mind to become a monk and forget all the troubles of mortal life.

The reunion of Tian Yuan and Su Shui can be consid-ered as the highlight of the dance drama. This couple, re-plete with conjugal love and having experienced all kinds of sufferings together, are well within each other's reach. However, they seem to be thousands of *li* apart. Seeing Tian Yuan's dilemma that he can't love his wife but is unwilling to part with her, and seeing Su Shui's heart-breaking sadness,

Bai Juyi (772-846) was born in Xinzheng County, Henan Province. Like Du Fu, he also had a strong sense of social responsibility, and he is also well-known for his satirical poems. Two of his most famous works are the long narrative poems "Song of Eternal Sorrow", which tells the story of Concubine Yang Yuhuan, and "Song of the Pipa Player". He wrote over 3,000 poems, brief, topical verses ex-pressed in very simple, clear language. He held the view that good poetry should be readily understood by the common people and exemplified it in poems noted for simple diction, natural style, and social content.

Li Shangyin (also known as Li Yishan) (813-858), was a Chinese poet of the late Tang Dynasty, born in Henei (now Qinyang, Henan Province). Li was a typical Late Tang poet: his works are sensuous, dense and allusive. He was much ad-mired for the imagist quality of his poems. His *Jinti* poems (modern style poem),

we are moved to tears. As the composer of the music in this dance drama, Tang Jianping's musical talent is brought into full play here. The touching and plaintive tune renders people's tears trickling down their checks.

If we can say the martial art of *Shaolin in the Wind* displays the heroic nature of this land,

If we can say the dance of *Shaolin in the Wind* reflects the poetic local tradition and customs,

If we can say the stage of *Shaolin in the Wind* reproduces the abundant culture deposit,

We can claim that the music of *Shaolin in the wind* gives a miraculous sketch of the spirit of this land.

From the soul-stirring and vigorous tune, we hear clearly rough but charming Henan *bangzi* (a kind of opera in Henan Province performed to the accompaniment of wooden clappers), and deep and fervent Yellow River *haozi* (a working song sung to synchronize movement).

From the lingering sound in this magnificent scene, we hear pure, mellow sound of the chimes of old cities of Zheng and Han states in the Warring States Period.

And from the music, we hear the familiar sound of the

especially *Qilü* (eight-line Chinese classical poem with seven characters to a line), boast a unique style, contributing a lot to the development of artistic form.

Buddha and Love

"Buddha" is a state and the inner love characteristic of extremely strong interactivity.

This love, stemming from the inner heart, enjoying a long origin, rooted in holiness and spread all over the world, en-

郑州出土的唐代佛像　Statues of Buddhas of the Tang Dynasty Unearthed in Zhengzhou

three-stringed plucked instrument and *suona* (a traditional
Chinese musical instrument), and intimate folk songs and
canzonets.

All these are all the songs of nature of this land.

When Tian Yuan drops the handkerchief which wit-
nessed their affection, we don't know whether we should sym-
pathize with him or blame him. But as to Tian Yuan, he seems
to have completed his conversion.

For the enlightened,
Hardly any obstacles stand in the way to Buddhism.
When love and hatred vanish together,
Everything seems to become clear
And shows its nature.
Now we can see the nuance,
Existing between the heaven and the earth.

compasses all living creatures.

This love, focusing on giving, diligent in spreading, ignorant of the gain and
loss, disregarding rewards, delivers all living creatures from the torments in this
world.

As for Buddha or love, no matter whether the result is refusal or acceptance,
so long as there is Buddha and love in one's heart, that's enough. If one's love is
accepted by the other, it can be called mutual love; and if one's love is refused, it
can't be said that they are doomed to part with each other. As to "Buddha", the
refusal of love may be the giving and acceptance of a deeper love.

Love is sweet but painful. Love is human's everlasting pursuit and life's eternal theme. People are born for love; people feel proud, painful and distressed for
love; people love and hate for love.

There are different kinds of love. Ordinary love is a kind of giving, the motive of which is receiving. It's also a kind of receiving, the prerequisite of which is giving. However, Buddha's love is a kind of giving, but a selfless one; it is a kind of receiving, but a tolerant one.

Folk Songs in Zhengzhou

From the discovery of the seven-hole *xun* (an ancient musical instrument) of the New Stone Age, and the set of bells (or chimes) of the Warring States Period which can produce high and low intervals of musical notes, to the archetypes of various musical instruments in Gongyi grottoes of the Northern Wei Dynasty, the musical performances carved on the stone relieves of the Han Dynasty, the performance of the dancers' figures of the Tang Dynasty, and the festively singing and dancing performers of the Song Dynasty, all of these invariably narrate the long standing history of music and art in Zhengzhou region.

In *Odes of Zheng*, which is one part of *Book of Odes*, the lyrics of 21 popular folk songs have been reserved. It is a pity that the music scores have fallen into oblivion in the long river of history. Fortunately, there are still some folk songs handed down from mouth to mouth, emerging and perishing naturally, thus carrying on the melody of remote antiquity.

According to the theme and singing manner, the folksongs in Zhengzhou

can be classified into fisherman's songs, the folksongs sung in the fields or in mountain areas, canzonets, singing and dancing canzonets, ballads and nursery dongs, etc.

Among them are songs reflecting work and production, namely the Yellow River boatmen's chant, rammers' work chant, porters' chant, etc. Although the current of the Yellow River at Zhengzhou, Gongyi and Xingyang is calm, the rhythm of the boatmen's chant is loud and sonorous, flowing and ringing unrestrainedly. The rhythm of the rammers' chant in Xinmi, Xinzheng and Gongyi is smooth and powerful, brief and clear, bold and natural. Besides, porters have their own chants to encourage each other. Usually a chant is led by one person, while the others sing in a chorus. More often than not, apart from simple chanting, the lyrics in a chant are impromptu, humorous and optimistic, which help eliminate tiredness and make their pace of labor in harmony. Such a chant usually has regular rhythm, with few rises and falls, suitable for singing and spreading.

There are relatively a greater number of canzonets among different kinds of folksongs in Zhengzhou. The canzonets usually have complete and stable scores and lyrics. The rhythm of them is elegant and graceful, sweet and pleasant to the ear. Good examples include "Antistrophic Songs on Flowers", and "Flying Kites", etc., which reflect people's thoughts and feelings in their work and life. In addition, songs sung in the field, religious songs and nursery songs are also widely spread folksongs.

Five traditional Chinese musical tones are all adopted in the folksongs of Zhengzhou, namely, *Gong, Shang, Jue, Zhi,* and *Yu.* The musical tones of *Zhi* and *Gong* are most frequently used. Different musical scales are used, especially the penta-tonic scale, in many folksongs, thus forming a style of fluid and smooth tone, and of soft and graceful melody.

Notes:

1. Gong, Shang, Jue, Zhi, and Yu: Basic five notes of the ancient Chinese five-tone scale, corresponding to 1, 2, 3, 5, 6 respectively in numbered musical notation.

Fan is a note of the scale, corresponding to 4 in numbered musical notation.

2. Chinese music is basically pentatonic-diatonic, meaning that the basic pentatonic scale can be modulated within a diatonic context. The theory talks of 12-notes to an octave, but most of the compositions are overwhelmingly pentatonic with diatonic/chromatic passing tones.

风中 舞 动少林
SHAOLIN:
DANCING
IN THE WIND

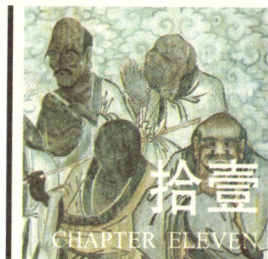

拾壹
CHAPTER ELEVEN

失去天元的素水也失去了自己的生命。

当中原再遭生灵涂炭之时，素水又张开自己美丽的臂膀，捧出对生养自己的这片土地更深的爱……

罪恶的黑手折断了天鹅美丽的翅膀。

素水倒地的一瞬，也绽放出生命的惊艳。

《风中少林》无处不在传递一种诗意、一种美：舞蹈的美、武术的美，风情的美、生命的美。

超度亡灵的梵歌中，也透着生命的美质——

神情肃穆的僧人们双目低垂，双手合十。

梦幻般的光环中，满台白色的身影带着人生的依恋，长袖飘飞，翩翩起舞。

一个生命的圆在袅袅娜娜中合拢，继而曼舞成一朵盛开的白莲，沐浴着清幽的梵唱，静静地舒展在忘忧河上，宁静而洁净！

君似佛莲花，刹那却永恒！

佛说：每个人都是佛前的一朵莲花，在五百年前，日日陪伴在佛祖身边，听佛祖讲人世沉浮，苦海无边。

就这样过了一世又一世，低头望尘寰，多了许多浮浮沉沉的离合悲欢。如今，还是佛前洁白的莲，亭亭静植，不忧也不惧，无悲亦无喜。

相关链接

莲花与佛

莲花是佛教的象征，佛教称莲花为"佛教圣花"。

当人们走进寺庙，抬头便可看见佛祖释迦牟尼身穿通肩大衣，手作说法印，结跏趺坐在莲花台上。佛经说，这是释迦佛祖修道成佛后向信徒们讲经说法的姿态。称为"西方三圣"之首的阿弥陀佛也结跏趺坐在莲台上，双掌仰置于足上，掌中托着一个莲台，似乎在指引众生通往西方佛国净土。以大慈大悲闻名的观音，更是身

穿白衣，坐在白莲花上，一手持着一只净瓶，一手执着一朵白莲，仿佛在表露观音怀着一颗纯洁的菩萨心，全力导引信徒脱离尘世，到达荷花盛开的佛国净土。

在翻读佛经时，人们又常常会见到佛经把佛国称为"莲界"，把寺庙称为"莲舍"，把和尚的袈裟称为"莲服"，把和尚行法手印称为"莲华合掌"，连和尚手中的念珠也是用莲子串成的。佛经说，用莲子作念珠比用槐木珠要好，同样掐念一遍，所得之福，可多千倍。

莲花与佛教结下了亲密的因缘，成了佛国的象征与圣花。佛教之所以如此崇拜荷花，简要地说有两方面原因：

第一，与荷花特性相关。荷花是一种多年生的水生植物花卉，她虽不像牡丹那样雍容华贵，也没有菊花那样的孤傲清高，但她出污泥而不染，迎骄阳而盛开，赢得了佛教至高无上的崇拜。佛教认为世间充满"六尘"，由于"六尘"的污染与干扰，人世间又充满着欲望与竞争，使人们难以平静，难得洁净。这种情况与"远尘离垢，得法眼净"的佛国净土是格格不入的。要想进入佛国，必须远离尘世，遁入清净的空门，专心修佛，消除污染与干扰。荷花出污泥而不染的特性与人世间的佛教信徒希望自己不受尘世污染的愿望是一致的。

第二，受到古印度崇拜荷花习俗的影响。早在佛教诞生以前的印度，每当夏天，烈日炎炎，而这正是荷花盛开的季节。夏夜，或清晨，在荷塘畔散步赏荷，粉红淡紫相间，赏心悦目。清风徐来，荷香随风从万绿丛中散发出来，令人的心肺像洗涤过似的顿觉凉爽。荷塘畔便成了避暑的胜地。

在印度佛经中，还将释迦牟尼的诞生与荷花联系起来。佛经中说：释迦降生之前，皇宫御苑中曾出现了八种瑞相，百鸟群集，鸣声相和悦耳，四季花卉一同盛开。尤为奇异的是，释迦牟尼降生时，宫内的大池塘中突然长出一朵大如车轮的白莲花。释迦牟尼降生之初，在舌根中又闪出千道金光，每一道金光又化作一朵千叶白莲，每朵莲花之中还坐着一位盘脚交叉、足心向上的小菩萨。

在印度的佛经中，荷花的分类也与佛教有关。以荷花

颜色分之，佛经上有白、青、红、紫、黄等五色，称为"五种天华"。这五种莲花，为五大虚空藏菩萨所坐，佛经上说：

东方福智虚空藏，坐青莲花，乘银牛；

南方能满虚空藏，坐赤莲花，乘金象；

西方施顾虚空藏，坐白莲花，乘琉璃马；

北方无垢虚空藏，坐紫莲花，乘狮子；

中央解脱虚空藏，坐黄金莲花，乘水晶龟。

还有以莲瓣多寡分之，佛经上说有人华、天华和菩萨华三种。人华者，莲瓣仅十余而已；天华者，莲瓣达数百；而菩萨华者，莲瓣多达千数，即是佛教最尊崇的千（瓣）莲花，佛国莲华的象征。

For Su Shui, losing Tian Yuan signifies the loss of her own life.

When the Central-China Plains are plunged into an abyss of misery again, Su Shui is stretching out her beautiful arms another time and offering her deeper love towards the land that has nurtured her.

The evil hands are breaking the swan's beautiful wings.

The moment Su Shui falls onto the ground, suddenly appears on the stage the splendor of life.

Every scene in *Shaolin in the Wind* conveys a sense of poetic flavor and beauty: the beauty of dance, martial art, local condition and customs as well as life.

The Buddhist songs that redeem the soul of a deceased person also transmit the beauty of life—the solemn monks drooping their eyelids and pressing the palms together.

Among the illusive rings of light, white figures on the stage are dancing trippingly with their long sleeves floating and flying, reluctant to part with earthly life.

Gradually, a circle signifying life is closing gently and gracefully, and then changing into a white lotus in full bloom,

Related Links

Lotus and Buddhism

Lotus is the symbol of Buddhism and is called "the holy flower of Buddhism".

In Buddhist sutras, all the three deities of the West, Shakyamuni, Amitabha and Budhisattva are portrayed to sit on lotus-thrones to preach to the sentimental beings. Buddhist countries, temples, kasayas and the monks' pressing the palms together are called "the world of lotus", "the residence of lotus", "the clothes of lotus" and "the pressing palms of lotus" respectively. The rosaries used by the monks are made from lotus seeds, which are regarded to be better than the ones made from pagoda wood. Pattering Buddhist sutras while twiddling a string of lotus rosaries will be blessed, and the blessing would be a thousand times more powerful than that with a string of pagoda-wood rosaries.

Lotus is closely related to Buddhism and becomes a symbol and the holy

bathed in the peaceful Buddhist songs and quietly unfolding herself in a river which could help people forget their worries, tranquil and pure.

Like the lotus for a Buddha, you are instantaneous but eternal.

Buddha says that everyone was one of the lotuses for Buddhas five hundred years ago, accompanying Buddha all the time and listening to the patriarch's sermons on the ups and downs and boundless sea of bitterness of one's mortal life.

Looking back to the mortal life which goes through one generation after another, it's always full of ups and downs and joys and sorrows. However, now the white and pure lotuses seated with Buddha, tall and straight, are beyond any care and fear, grievance and happiness.

flower in the Buddhist realm. There are two reasons as follows:

Firstly, it has something to do with the lotus' specific property. Being a kind of perennial aquatic flower, although not as elegant and poised as peony, and not as proud and aloof as chrysanthemum, a lotus stays uncontaminated even though growing in dirty mud, and it blooms under the scorching sun in the sultry summer. Such qualities of lotus win the worship of Buddhists. It is believed in Buddhist sutras that the world is filled with "six kinds of dust"; contaminated with and troubled by them, the mortal world is permeated with desire and competition which keep people far from being tranquil and pure; such condition is totally out of tune with the clean Buddhist realms, which are "away from dirt and dust". Hence wishing to enter the Buddhist realms, one must be away from the mortal world, living in the temple and meditating on Buddhism so as to dispel contamination and interference.

The specific property of lotus, not contaminated though living in dirty mud, is consistent with the wishes of the Buddhist disciples to be unpolluted by the mortal world.

Secondly, it is under the influence of the ancient Indian custom of worshiping the lotus. As early as before the appearance of Buddhism, lotus was the favorite flower of the Indian people. As we all know, summer in India is very hot. When in summer the sun was scorching, the Indian would take a walk along the bank of the lotus pond, for the delicate fragrance and beautiful scene would make them feel cool and comfortable.

Hence, in the Buddhist sutras of India, the birth of Shakyamuni is linked with the lotus: when Shakyamuni was about to be born, there appeared eight auspicious signs in the garden of the imperial palace. One is that all kinds of birds, whose songs were extremely pleasant to the ears, gathered together and sang in chorus. Another is that the flowers which should bloom in four different seasons were in full bloom at the same time. The most mystic and surprising thing is that at the moment of the birth of Shakyamuni, a white lotus as big as the wheel sprouted in the pond of the palace. When he was born, thousands of golden rays were sent out from his tongue, and then each of them changed into a lotus with a thousand petals and on each of the lotuses sat a cross-legged small bodhisattva whose soles were upward.

According to Sutra, the lotus has five colors, namely, white, blue, red, purple and yellow, called "five heavenly blossoms", in which white and blue are the two most esteemed. The five breeds of the lotus are for five Akasagarbhas to sit on respectively:

Blessing and wisdom Akasagarbha in the east, seated on the blue lotus, riding on the silver cattle;

Capacity full Akasagarbha in the south, seated on the red lotus, riding on the gold elephant;

Philanthropic and caring Akasagarbha in the west, seated on the white lotus, riding on the glaze horse;

Dirt-free Akasagarbha in the north, seated on the purple lotus, riding on the lion;

Mukti Akasagarbha in the center, seated on the golden lotus, riding on the crystal turtle.

The lotus can also be classified according to the number of its petals. In the Buddhist Sutras, there are human blossoms, heavenly blossoms and Bodhisattva's blossoms. Human blossoms refer to the lotus with just more than ten petals; heavenly blossoms refer to the lotus with hundreds of petals; while Bodhisattva's blossoms refer to the lotus with almost a thousand petals which is the most precious one-thousand-petal lotus and the symbol of lotus in the Buddhist heaven.

Notes:

White Lotus (Skt. pundarika; Tib. pad ma dkar po): This represents the state of spiritual perfection and total mental purity (bodhi). It is associated with the White Tara and proclaims her perfect nature, a quality which is reinforced by the color of her body.

Pink Lotus (Skt. padma; Tib. pad ma dmar po): This is the supreme lotus, generally reserved for the highest deity. Thus naturally it is associated with the Great Buddha himself.

Red Lotus (Skt. kamala; Tib. pad ma chu skyes): This signifies the original nature and purity of the heart (hrdya). It is the lotus of love, compassion, passion and all other qualities of the heart. It is the flower of Avalokiteshvara, the bodhisattva of compassion.

Blue Lotus (Skt. utpala; Tib. ut pa la): This is a symbol of the victory of the spirit over the senses, and signifies the wisdom of knowledge. Not surprisingly, it is the preferred flower of Manjushri, the bodhisattva of wisdom.

Each of the flowers is painted with two rows of five petals, just like a real lotus flower. The flowers are decorated with five different colors: red, green, blue, gold and silver. Of these five colors, silver is the only one which has worn off over time and is difficult to see.

风中 SHAOLIN: DANCING IN THE WIND 动少林

拾贰
CHAPTER TWELVE

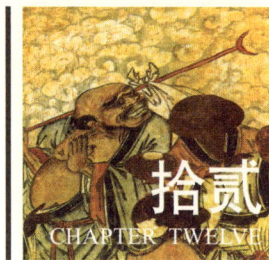

我们又看到慧山大师的身影,慈悲为怀的出家人用悲愤擂起讨伐的战鼓。

这是正义与邪恶的较量,这是法理与爱心的张扬。

这是一种雄性之美,一种力量之美,一种正气之美,一种大德之美。

隐忍并不是退让,慈悲并不是放纵。

大风起兮云飞扬——

挺身而出,回闪的是十三棍僧救唐王的壮举。

相 关 链 接

英雄少林

十三棍僧救唐王

公元620年,李世民率兵出关,同盘踞在洛阳自称郑王的王世充交战。战斗紧要关头,以昙宗为首的少林寺僧众操起棍棒,乘虚袭击了王世充后营,活捉了王世充的侄子王仁则,捆绑送至唐营。为酬谢少林众僧的战功,李世民登基后,"嘉其义烈,频降玺书宣慰。赐田四十顷,水碾一具",同时对十三位立功和尚各有嘉奖,昙宗被封为大将军。

少林寺白衣殿的十三僧救唐王壁画
Mural Paintings of Thirteen Shaolin Monks Fighting with Cudgels Rescuing Li Shimin，the 2nd Emperor of the Tang Dynasty

　　大义凛然，再现的是宗印法师抗击金兵、威镇中原的豪气。

　　鼓角齐鸣，翻开的是月空法师、小山和尚奉旨挂帅、抗击倭寇的历史。

　　吼声震天，荡起的是三奇和尚镇山陕的记忆……

宗印法师抗金

　　北宋末年，金兵南侵，占领了军事要地潼关，河南尹范致虚调少林寺武僧宗印为宣抚司参议兼节制军马，宗印把佛门僧众组成"尊胜队"和"净胜队"两军，亲率他们向潼关进发。国难当头，少林僧率兵出征，足以证明少林寺僧习武是为了制止争战，报效国家，普度苍生，救民水火。

　　退则参禅养性修道行,进则护寺报国救众生。就这样,在千年古刹的烽烟岁月中,一个个身怀绝技的少林武僧,用自己的血肉之躯和浩然正气,演绎了一曲曲扬善惩恶的人间传奇。

　　巍巍嵩岳,众山朝揖之宗;莽莽中州,万古英雄之气。

　　雄浑的嵩山,象征的正是这片英雄辈出的土地。

　　这是一块英豪辈出的土地。嵩山坚硬的岩石铸就了陈胜的铮铮铁骨,峻极峰顶的云霞辉耀着杜密流芳青史的一身正气,历史的烽烟中高扬着李际遇揭竿而起的大旗,中岳庙的铁人凝固着面对入侵者的满腔怒火……所有这些,都和着高亢豪迈的豫腔,在高天上放飞……

　　因此,在《风中少林》开始的时候,我们有理由期待在这个少林武僧的传奇里找到历史的身影!

紧那罗王御红巾

　　元朝末年,少林寺曾与红巾军对抗。据说,红巾军攻少林寺时,烧火僧人紧那罗手持烧火棍而出,变形十丈,脚立两座山峰之上,大叫"吾紧那罗王也",吓退了红巾军。后来,少林寺武僧把紧那罗王尊为"二辈师爷",说他是棍术大师,并把他看作少林寺的护法神。今天少林寺僧人习练的棍法中还有一路"烧火棍法",据说就是紧那罗王传下的。少林寺大雄宝殿的东面,还建有面向西的紧那罗殿,内塑三尊4米高的持棍护法、妙法、持法紧那罗像,供后人祭祀。

Picture of King Jinnaluo　紧那罗王像

月空法师抗倭

明朝中期，东南沿海经常受到倭寇侵扰，"本寺武僧屡经调遣，奋勇杀敌，屡立战功"。少林月空法师接到都督万表的檄文，立即带领三十多个武僧奔赴松江一带抵御倭寇，战斗中僧兵个个奋勇，用铁棒击杀倭寇甚多，后来他们全都壮烈牺牲在战场上。明末爱国思想家顾炎武曾在《少林僧兵》一文中大加赞扬。小山和尚也曾三次挂帅出征。嘉靖三十二年（1553年），明朝又调参公和尚率僧兵五十多人赴东南沿海作战。后来万庵、便公和尚也都应征作战，立过战功，郑若曾《僧兵首捷记》中说："夫今之武艺，天下莫不让少林焉。"在各路兵马中少林寺僧"最为骁勇"，于是声名大振，少林武术被大家一致公认为武林泰斗、天下第一大门派。抗倭名将戚继光在《纪效新书》中把少林棍法列为全国棍法的佼佼者。

三奇和尚镇山陕

三奇是少林寺一位战功显赫的僧兵。他原名周友，在正德年间"蒙钦取宣调"，镇守山东、陕西布政使司(省)辖下的堡塞，御封为"都提调总兵"，并曾奉命统征云南，讨伐叛蛮。塔林中现存有"三奇友公和尚塔"，方形，单层三檐。塔额曰："敕赐大少林禅寺，教名'天下对手，教会武僧'……赏友公三奇和尚之寿塔。"其中所说赏为"三奇和尚"，就是说他是立过三次"奇功"的和尚。永乐以后，分军功为三等，即奇功、首功、次功。周友获得三次奇功，可见其英勇善战，武艺高超。

嵩岳壮歌

距今4000年到3000年，嵩山地区是夏商周三代立国的中心，禹都阳城，启都阳翟、斟寻，汤都西亳，商都郑州，东都洛邑环嵩山而立，嵩山在中国文化史上居有不可取代的中心地位。大禹是嵩山第一位传奇英雄，大禹治水改堵为疏，劈九山，通九泽，决九川，治服洪水，又划九州，铸九鼎，定都阳城，安定天下。

秦朝末年，刑法严苛，统治残暴，胸怀鸿鹄之志的登封阳城人陈胜，"伐无道，诛暴秦"，率先举起反秦义旗，动摇了秦王朝的统治，并建立了我国历史上第一个农民政权"张楚"。

西汉时，阳城矿工申屠圣因不满铁官迫害，也奋而起义，虽然以失败告终，但却是中国历史上第一次工人起义。

东汉末年，宦官专政，朝政黑暗，登封人杜密，刚正不阿，廉洁奉公，执法严明，得罪不少官宦。因党

Statue of Da Yu at Mount Mang in Zhengzhou 郑州邙山大禹塑像

锢之祸免归家乡后，他仍然知善即荐，闻恶必言，后终丧身于党锢之祸。杜密被太学生们誉为"天下良辅杜周甫"，和曾隐居阳城的名士李膺并称"李杜"。

　　明朝末年，嵩山大旱，颗粒无收，百姓饥寒交迫，李际遇揭竿而起，聚众起义，杀登封知县鄢廷诲。义军发展到四五万人，后加入闯王李自成的军队，席卷豫西十几个县。

陈胜吴广起义图 Picture of the 1st Peasant Uprising Led by Chen Sheng and Wu Guang

On the stage appears again the silhouette of Master Hui Shan, the benevolent monk beating the drum of crusade against the suppressors with grief and indignation.

This is a fight of justice against villainy, publicizing legal principle and love.

Lies in it is the beauty of masculine courage, gallantry, strength, righteousness and great virtue.

Forbearance is not giving in, and benevolence is not indulging.

A great wind rises, oh! The clouds are driven away.

What flashes before us is the heroic feat of the thirteen Shaolin monks who came out boldly to rescue and aid Emperor Taizong of the Tang Dynasty in suppressing a rebellion led by Wang Shichong.

It reappears before us the heroic spirit of master Zong Yin who fought against the troups from Jin with stern righteousness, whose name was remembered in the Central-China Plains.

When battle drums were beaten and horns blown, the history of master Yue Kong and monk Xiao Shan who took command by order of the emperor to fight against the Japa-

Related Links

Heroes of Shaolin Buddhist Monastery

Thirteen Shaolin Monks Fighting with Cudgels Rescuing Li Shimin

In 620 A.D., Li Shimin, king of the Qin state, fought with the self-appointed emperor of the Zheng state, Wang Shichong. Shaolin monks Zhi Cao, Hui Yang, and Tan Zong took the side of Li and helped him catch the latter's nephew Wang Renze to force the self-appointed emperor to surrender. After Li Shimin was enthroned as the 2nd emperor of the Tang Dynasty, he awarded his followers according to their military merits and contributions. Monk Tan Zong had the title of chief general conferred on him, while Shaolin Buddhist Monastery was given large grants of land and money to expand the temple complex. Shaolin Buddhist Monastery was allowed to organize an army of monk soldiers, who acted as military

nese pirates, was laid open.

In the howl of defending, the memories of monk San Qi (meaning "three outstanding meritorious deeds"), who took the lead of monk soldiers and fought bravely to guard the fortress under the administration of Shandong and Shaanxi, were recollected.

The age-old mission of the Shaolin sect of martial art is "to cultivate Ch'an Buddhism during times of peace, and to defend the temple, the country and the people during times of war". Thus during its one-thousand-year history, many Shaolin martial monks , with their unique skills, their bodies of flesh and blood, their grand righteousness, have composed many a legendary story of poetical justice in which evil people were punished and righteousness was spread.

The towering Mt. Song is the ancestral mountain worshiped by other mountains. The innumerable legends of heroes spread in the Central-China Plains.

The imposing Mt. Song symbolizes the land where numerous heroes display their heroic spirit in history. This is the land where many a hero was born. The hard rocks of Mt.

people in warring times and as monks in time of peace.

Monk-saint Zong Yin Fighting Against Jin Soldiers

At the end of the Northern Song Dynasty, Jin soldiers invaded south China and they occupied an important military fort, Tongguan. The imperial official of Henan Province appointed Zong Yin the commander. Zong Yin divided the monk soldiers into two teams, namely *Zunsheng* Team and *Jingsheng* Team. Led by Zong Yin, the two teams left for Tongguan. When the nation was in crisis, the monks went out to battle. This clearly shows that the nature for Shaolin monks to practice Kung Fu is to stop the war, serve the country, liberate all living creatures from torment and save the people from fire and water.

Notes: Jin Dynasty (1115 A.D.-1234 A.D., founded by Akutta, chieftain of the Nü -zhen tribes, with nine emperors in the reign of the northern part of China for 120 years.)

Song cast Chen Sheng's firm and unyielding bones; the rosy clouds on the top of the mountain glorified Du Mi, who has left a good name in the annals of history; flying in the beacon fire of history was the big flag raised by Li Jiyu for his standard of revolt; and standing in Zhongyue Temple were the iron men having their bosoms filled with rage against invaders. All these best demonstrate the top melody of heroic spirit in Henan Province.

Therefore, when the dance drama *Shaolin in the Wind* begins, we have good reasons to expect a personal experience of history in the pathetically eventful life of a military monk of Shaolin Buddhist Monastery.

King Jinnaluo defeating Red Scarf Army

At the end of the Yuan Dynasty, monks of Shaolin Buddhist Monastery fought against the Red Scarf Army. It is said that, when the Red Scarf Army attacked Shaolin Buddhist Monastery, a fire monk named Jinnaluo, who was responsible to tend the kitchen fire, came out with a poker in his hand. With his figure transferred into a ten-*zhang* (unit of length, a *zhang*=3.3 meters) tall giant and his two feet standing at the top of two hills, he shouted: "I'm the King Jinnaluo". Hearing that, the Red Scarf Army was terribly frightened and withdrew. Later, Shaolin monks honored King Jinnaluo as the second-generation master as well as the master of cudgel fighting. He was also honored to be the god of preserving Buddhism in Shaolin Buddhist Monastery. In today's cudgel skills, there exists one called "fire cudgel fighting" which is still practiced by Shaolin monks, and it is said that it has been passed on from King Jinnaluo. To the east of the Daxiong Hall in Shaolin Buddhist Monastery, there is the Hall of King Jinnaluo facing the west. In the hall, there are three statues of King Jinnaluo in different poses for people after him to offer sacrifices.

Monk-saint Yue Kong Fighting Against Japanese Pirates

In the middle of the Ming Dynasty, the coastal areas in southeast China were frequently invaded by Japanese pirates. The Shaolin monks in the Ming Dynasty (1368-1644) were all taught to practise Wushu. In the 32nd calendar year of the Jiajing reign (1553), the Shaolin martial monks took part in the battles against Japanese invaders in south China and accomplished many military exploits.

Responding to the official call to arms given by the provincial military governor Wanbiao, Master Yue Kong led Shaolin martial monks to go to Song Jiang and its nearby places immediately to fight against Japanese pirates. During the battles, the brave monks killed many a Japanese pirate with iron sticks. But unfortunately all of them were killed at the end. The patriotic thinker Gu Yanwu sung high praise of them in his book *Shaolin Monk Soldiers*. Monk Xiao Shan also commanded Shaolin martial monks to battle for three times. More monks were recruited into the army and they distinguished themselves in action. In his book *The First Victory of Monk Soldiers*, Zheng Ruozeng said, "In respect to today's martial art, Shaolin tops the list". Among the armies from different parts of the country, Shaolin monks were the "bravest soldiers". Shaolin martial art attained great reputation all over the country and were unanimously regarded as the most famous as well as the No. I School of martial art. In his book, Qi Jiguang, a patriotic general famous for his fighting against Japanese pirates, said that Shaolin cudgel fighting skills are the best in the country.

Monk San Qi Guarded the Fortress

Monk San Qi (meaning "three outstanding meritorious deeds") was a famous monk soldier with outstanding military exploit. His original name was Zhou You. During the reign period of Zhengde (the reign title of Emperor Wuzong in the Ming Dynasty), he was assigned by the imperial government to guard an important fortress. He took the lead of monk soldiers and fought bravely to guard the fortress under the imperial administration of Shandong and Shaanxi Provinces. Later, he led the army to battle in Yunnan and fight against the armed rebellious troop. Currently existing in the pagoda forest of Shaolin Buddhist Monastery is a tower built in honor of him. It is in square shape, and it has one storey and three eaves. Carved on the forehead of the tower are "Bestowed with the Grand Shaolin Buddhist Monastery... Built for San Qi, Granted with the title of Master Military Monk". San Qi is a title granted to him to praise his three outstanding meritorious deeds in battle. In Chinese history, after the reign period of Yongle (the reign title of Emperor Chengzu of the Ming Dynasty), military merits were divided into three levels: outstanding merit, first merit and second merit. Monk Zhou You attained three outstanding merits, which best manifested his brave and skillful fighting in battle as well as his superb martial art.

Heroic Undertakings of Mount Song

About 3,000 to 4,000 years ago, the region around Mt. Song was the central area for three dynasties, namely, the Xia, the Shang and the Zhou Dynasties, to build their capitals. Yangcheng was built as the capital by King Yu, Yangzhai and Zhenxun by King Qi of the Xia Dynasty, West Bo by King Tang of the early Shang Dynasty. Zhengzhou was made the capital of the Shang Dynasty, and Luoyi the east capital. These capitals formed a circle surrounding Mt. Song, thus establishing its irreplaceable position as the center in Chinese cultural history. Great Yu, King of the Xia Dynasty, is the first legendary hero of Mt. Song. In order to regulate rivers and watercourses, he used the method of dredging rather than blocking up. He cleaved nine hills, broke nine pools, and brought nine rivers under control. Also, it is Great Yu who conquered the flood and divided the country into nine divisions and cast nine *dings* (*ding*: tripod cauldron for cooking, with three legs and two ears). He made Yangcheng the capital of the Xia Dynasty and there settled his people. Through Chinese history, stories of righteous deeds have been continued and passed on generation after generation.

At the end of the Qin Dynasty, people lived in the threat of strict corporal punishment and cruel rule. Chen Sheng, a strongly ambitious man from Dengfeng, Zhengzhou, put forward the call to "strike the unprincipled ruler, and put to death the cruel emperor" with stern determination. As a pioneer to fight against the reign of the Qin Dynasty, he started the prelude of the first peasant uprising which shocked the ruling foundation of the Qin Dynasty. Later, he established the first regime by peasants, and it was named "Zhangchu" in history.

In the Western Han Dynasty, being unsatisfied with persecutions from the officials, Shen Tusheng, a miner from Yangcheng, began to uprise with anger. Although he failed in the end, his struggle turns out to be the first one for miners to uprise in Chinese history.

At the end of the Eastern Han Dynasty, eunuch dictatorship prevailed in the country. The court administration was totally dark. Du Mi, an upright and honest man who hated flattery, performed his official duties and enforced the law strictly, offended a lot of eunuchs. After he was dismissed out of party sanction and went back home, he still recommended virtuous people to serve in the court and reveal evil things after hearing them. Finally he failed to escape from the threat of party sanction and was killed for his deeds. Du Mi was honorably reputed as "the best instructor of the country" by students from the Imperial College. Together with another celebrity named Li Ying, who lived in seclusion in Yangcheng, the two of them were called "Li and Du" in history. Du Mi therefore left a good reputation in history because of his righteousness. Mt. Song was the place that formed his personality. In turn, the cultural history of Mt. Song has become more glorious thanks to his reputation.

In the Song Dynasty when the famous general Yue Fei's army was fighting against invaders of the Jin Dynasty who occupied north China, the general once stationed his troops at Zhongyue Temple and planned for the final battle at the town of Zhuxian. Legend has it that when Yue Fei left for the town of Zhuxian, the iron men in the temple were deeply moved, and they also prepared to join the army. They failed to cross the Yellow River and were carried back by Taoist priests from the temple. Today, the four iron men are still regretful for their failure, and they are still filled with indignation, staring at each other in great anger.

At the end of the Ming Dynasty, severe drought threatened the area of Mt. Song, which suffered from a total crop failure. People lived in starvation and cold. However, the local government still exploited people mercilessly and urged them to turn in crops and money. A man called Li Jiyu couldn't bear it any more and raised the standard of revolt. He led people to rebel against the suppression and killed the local governor—Yan Tinghui. The rebellious army soon developed into a huge group of forty to fifty thousand people. Later, they joined the army headed by Li Zicheng (a rebel in late Ming China who proclaimed himself Chuang Wang [闯王], or "The Roaming King") and their fighting swept across more than ten counties in the western part of Henan Province.

Iron Statue of Shaolin Martial Monk in Wenbo Square in Zhengzhou　郑州文博广场上的少林武僧铁像

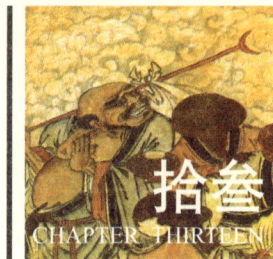

风中鄬动少林
SHAOLIN: DANCING IN THE WIND

拾叁
CHAPTER THIRTEEN

在震山撼岳的大对决中，凶残的强寇彻底化作了齑粉。

这是一个人们预料之中的结局。然而，并没有人指责大团圆的俗套，相反，在结局到来的时候，人们却是那么振奋，那么欣喜，那么扬眉吐气，那么酣畅淋漓……

是舞武结合营造的这场力感、动感、质感与美感兼具的"舞武盛宴"，给了观众太多的惊喜。

是世世代代炎黄儿女的骨子里刻印着佛教"因果业报"的痕迹：

相关链接

佛教的因果业报

因果，或称因果律，为佛教教义系统中用来说明世界一切关系的基本理论。谓一切事物皆由因果法则支配之，有因必有果，有果必有因，"已作不失，未作不得"。若否认这种因果之理的存在，则称"拔无因果"。《地藏轮经》云："拔无因果，断灭善根。"

佛教在因果问题上反对四种邪执：（1）邪因邪果，即将万物生起的原因归结为大自在天等超人格的力量。（2）无因有果，即承认现存的现象世界为果，但此果的原因是难以探究的，故否定此果的起因。（3）有因无果，即承认现存的现象世界为因，但此因的结果是难以探究的，故否定此因的结果。（4）无因无果，即

善有善报，恶有恶报，不是不报，时候不到，时候一到，必定要报。

千百年来，这是引领众生向善向美的动力……

精诚所至，金石为开。

天元脱下身上白色的战袍，以一身耀眼的橘红，迎着满台盛开的莲花，终于走向了禅宗圣祖。

凤凰涅槃，需要烈火的洗礼。

出世悟禅，更需世俗的磨难。

否定因果二者，不承认一切因果。

佛教认为，众生的行为能引生异时之因果，善之业因必有善之果报，恶之业因必有恶之果报，此称善因善果、恶因恶果，或称善因乐果、恶因苦果。这种因果之理称为因果业报，又作因果报应、善恶业报。若从实践修行上论因果关系，则由修行之因能招感成佛之果，这称为修因得果、修因感果。又一般所谓三世因果，多系指异熟因和异熟果之因果关系而言。亦即认为现世之罪福苦乐，乃前世所造善恶诸业的果报；而今生之善恶行为，亦必将影响来生的罪福报应。《因果经》云："欲知过去因者，见其现在果；欲知未来果者，见其现在因。"与三世因果密切相关的是三时报业。所谓三时报业，即根据善恶业因所招感异熟果的时间，分

厚重的岩壁轰然中开，走过了私欲情爱、悲欢离合，走过了山河破碎、生灵涂炭的天元，在佛光的引领下，步入了他心中的永恒……

风啸少林，逝去了恩怨情仇。

风舞少林，吹走了世俗纷争。

在天元双手合十，慢慢转身的一瞬，他的神情折射的是一种平和，一种宁静，一颗慈悲为怀的不动心——

让信义正气相伴大同盛世，

愿禅宗圣祖护佑一生平安……

少林寺千佛殿壁画
Mural Paintings in the Hall of Thousand Buddhas in Shaolin Buddhist Monastery

为：（1）顺现业，即现在世造业，现在世受报。（2）顺生业，即此世所造业，下一世受报。（3）顺后业，指此生所造业，在多世以后受报。《大宝积经》云："假使经百劫，所作业不亡，因缘会遇时，果报还自受。"

对因、缘、果具体分析，佛教有六因、四缘、五果之说。六因即能作因、俱有因、同类因、相应因、遍行因、异熟因；四缘即因缘、等无间缘（又称"次第缘"）、所缘缘、增上缘；五果即异熟果（又称"报果"）、等流果、士用果（又称"士夫果"）、增上果、离系果（又称"解脱果"）。

与因缘果报密切相关的一个概念是业。业，音译作"羯磨"，造作之义。意谓行为、作用、意志等身心活动。若与因果关系结

带着一种心灵沐浴的快感，《风中少林》在缓缓落幕……

透过纱幕上那块曾经无数次给人震撼的峭岩，厚重的皱褶如同历史的缝隙，依然有风在透出，不绝如缕——

禅如风，武如风，

这片土地的风情如风……

风中传送着英雄的情怀，

风中咏叹着生命的爱意，

风中歌咏着天下大同的精义……

合，则指由过去行为延续下来所形成的力量。善恶之业有生起苦乐之果的力用，称为业力。业的果报，则称业报，又称业果，即善恶业因招致的苦乐果报。业，本为印度自古流行的一个重要思想，佛教继承并发展了这一思想，作为佛法的重要内容。

需要指出的是，佛教

少林寺千佛殿壁画　Mural Paintings in the Hall of Thousand Buddhas in Shaolin Buddhist Monastery

虽然强调因果法则是普遍的宇宙规律，但并不承认宿命论。佛教在强调业力的同时，也充分肯定心力的作用。认为心能造业，心也能转业，业力与心力是相互作用的。《优婆塞戒经·业品》云："遇善知识，修道修善，是人能转后世重罪现世轻受。"《宗喀巴显密次第科颂》云："业果若不定，便成无因果；业果若决定，众生不成佛。当知业可转，如二水相投：热多冷从热，冷多热从冷。"彻悟禅师云："业由心造，业随心转。"

《风中少林》评述

哪里有改革，哪里就有新局面；创新是不竭的源泉；要面向市场、面向群众，走商业化演出的道路。这台舞剧把武术和舞蹈很好地结合在了一起，非常具有中原特色，哪一出戏的武打都没有这出戏好！

——中共中央政治局常委 李长春

《风中少林》无论从内容到形式，都有很多创新，是近年来少有的一台好戏。整个剧目文武结合，刚柔并济，以情动人、以舞感人、以技惊人，达到了观赏性与艺术性的统一。

——中共河南省委书记、河南省人大常委会主任 徐光春

如此震撼的恢宏场面所张扬的少林雄风，是当下舞剧里少见和需要的。其中武与舞结合的探索也是有价值的。

——文化部艺术司司长 于 平

这台舞剧可谓精心设计、精心制作、精心表演，令人激动、令人震撼。

——中国舞协名誉主席 贾作光

当我看到这个舞剧就觉得舞剧进入了新的里程碑。

——中国舞协副主席 赵 青

出乎我的意料，非常好看，有张力，有深度，舞蹈与武术的结合有创新意义，是中国舞剧舞台上的一朵奇葩。

——中国音协分党组书记、著名作曲家 徐沛东

2005—2006年度国家舞台艺术精品工程十大精品剧目评语：

　　本年度入选精品剧目的另一特点是都能勇敢探索并创新艺术元素乃至艺术样式，使舞台风貌和表演技巧与时俱进。舞剧《风中少林》取材于家喻户晓的少林武功故事，但其将舞蹈与武术结合起来，情节熔爱情、禅武、修炼、惩恶扬善的正义复仇于一炉，显示了很强的艺术综合性。

　　本年度入选精品剧目也受到了观众的热烈欢迎，取得了很好的市场效果。杂技剧《天鹅湖》和舞剧《风中少林》都取得了很好的社会和经济效益。《风中少林》已在境内外演出了75场，总收入达到1127万元。

Sweat and tears, just for the beautiful moment of a graceful capriole...　　汗水和泪水，为了那轻盈跃起的美丽一瞬……

In the decisive battle that could shock the mountains and hills, fierce and cruel enemies were defeated into pieces. Such an ending is not beyond people's expectation. However, nobody would criticize this conventional form of great reunion. On the contrary, when the ending comes, people are greatly inspired, full of rejoicing. They feel proud and elated, heartily enjoying the performance...

Such a perfect union of dance and Wushu gives people more than pleasant surprise, in which strength, action, quality and beauty are perfectly united.

Generation after generation, descendents of the Fire Emperor and the Yellow Emperor have engraved themselves with the law of cause and effect from Buddhism. Good will be rewarded with good, and evil with evil; if the reward is not forthcoming, it is because the time has not yet come; when time comes, all will get their due reward.

For thousands of years, this is the motivation which leads people to goodness and beauty.

Complete sincerity can affect even metal and stone.

When Tian Yuan takes off his white war robe, faced with lotuses in full blossom on the stage, he goes to the grand

Related Links
Law of Cause and Effect—*hetu-phala* in Buddhism

The law of cause and effect—*hetu-phala* is the essential theoretics in the whole system of Buddhist teachings, aiming at illuminating all the connections in the world. Everything in the world is dominated by this law. Cause and effect are mutually influential to each other. The denial of this law will lead one to "cut off the good roots", as stated in *Ti-tsang(Kshitigarbha) Sutra of Cakras*.

Four kinds of evil conducts (stubborn and wrongful opinions) are opposed in Buddhism in respect of hetu-phala. (1) Evil cause and evil effect: believing that super-natural power is the cause of the existence of all the living things on the earth; (2) Effect without cause: believing that the presently existent reality is the effect, but the cause is hard to explore, thus denying the cause of the effect; (3) Cause without effect: believing that the presently existent reality is the cause, but

master in bright orange.

Phoenix nirvana needs baptism in raging fire.

To perform meditation and realize Ch'an in the temple needs secular suffering to a greater degree.

When the thick and heavy cliffs are suddenly split open in halves, Tian Yuan has gone through selfish desire and love affairs, joys and sorrows, partings and reunions. He had seen the country when it was broken and his people were plunged into the abyss of misery. Finally, under the leading of Buddhist light, he enters the place of eternity.

Wind whistles in Shaolin Buddhist Monastery, and many feelings, sentiment and revenges pass away.

Wind dances in Shaolin Temple, secular disputes are blown away.

When Tian Yuan puts his palms together, and turns around slowly, a heart, peaceful and tranquil with stern benevolence, is reflected in his expressions.

Let trust and righteousness accompany our prosperous society in great harmony.

Wish the sacred Buddhist Patriarchs bless all of us with a peaceful life.

---

the effect is hard to explore, thus denying the effect brought about by the cause; (4) No cause and no effect: denying both sides, and denying all the cause-effect relations in the world.

It is believed in Buddhism that the actions of all flesh will naturally lead to certain results at another time. Good will be rewarded with good, and evil with evil; if the reward is not forthcoming, it is because the time has not yet come; when the time comes, one will get one's due reward. In regard of the practice of Buddhist cultivation, hetu-phala refers to the so-called "the cause and effect of three life times", esp. the cause-effect relation between *vipakahetu* and *vipaka-phala*. It means that the blessings and sufferings in this life are the results of the good and evil deeds in preexistence, and the good and evil deeds in this life will decide the blessings and sufferings in the other life, as it is said in *Saleyyaka Sutra*. There are

With a great sensation of pleasure like giving a bath to the soul, audiences see the ringing down of the curtains of *Shaolin in the Wind*...

On the stage, the huge steep rock, which has strikingly moved the audience for many times, is covered with many heavy folds resembling the great moments in history. Through them, gentle wind is still penetrating the curtains and stirring us incessantly.

The wind resembles Ch'an; the wind resembles Wushu,

The wind also resembles the local traditions and customs in this land...

The wind coveys the heroic sprit.

The wind sings highly of love in life.

The wind pays a tribute to the essence of universal harmony...

three times of *vipakas* (rewards): *vipakas* in this life, *vipakas* in the other life, and *vipakas* in a remote generation which may be 1,000 years later.

As for the concrete analysis of *hetu, pratyaya* and *phala*, there are six *hetus*, four *pratyayas* and five *phalas* in Buddhism. Six *hetus* include *karanahetu, sahabhuhetu, sabhagahetu, samprayuktakahetu, sarvatragahetu*, and *vipakahetu*. Four *pratyayas* include *hetupratyaya, samanantarapratyaya, alambanapratyaya,* and *adhipatipratyaya*. Five *phalas* include *vipaka-phala, adhipati-phala, nisyanda-phala, purusakara-phala,* and *visamyoga-phala*.

Closely related to *hetu-phala* is another concept, karma. It refers to the actions, effects and the will of one's body and mind. If combined with *hetu-phala*, it can be understood as the force accumulated from the past deeds. This force will help one to deal with the sufferings and happiness, which are the effect of good and evil doings. Originally karma was an important and popular ideology in ancient India. It has been inherited and developed by Buddhism and finally becomes an essential part of the power of Buddha.

What needs to be pointed out is that although the law of cause and effect is emphasized in Buddhism as the universal law, it denies fatalism. While emphasizing karma (internal power), Buddhism also fully acknowledges the function of mental efforts. It holds that mental efforts can help produce karma, and also can be converted into karma. There is obvious reciprocity between them. It says in *Saddharmapundarika Sutra*: "If one cultivates oneself according to the Buddhist doctrine, and tries one's best to be inclined to goodness, the severe sufferings, which would come in the other life, could be lessened in this life." In Master Tsong-kha-pa's *Classifications & Verses on the Steps of the Way to Bodhi*, it says:"If karma is indeterminate, it would be an effect without cause; if karma is determinate, all flesh wouldn't become Buddha. One must know that karma is convertible. It's just like the mixture of hot and cold water: the water will become hot if there is more hot water than cold water, and vice versa." A Buddhist monk named Che Wu (meaning: fully recognizing the truth) says: "Karma is produced by one's mind and can be converted by mental efforts."

Notes:

1. This is a lesson in karma, that we are ultimately responsible for our actions (also called the Law of Cause and Effect). If we can learn from a punishment and attain true rehabilitation, we rejoin the path and move ahead.

2. Karma is a very specific term in Asian thought, and is a measure of debt or accumulation that impedes the advancement of the spirit to a higher level. There is no such thing as "good" karma in Asia; one either acquires karma (not good) or eliminates it (the goal of meditation).

Comments on *Shaolin in the Wind*

Where there is a reform, there is new situation and continuous innovation. Art should be suited to the needs of market and people, and it should take the road of commercial performance. This dance drama is a perfect union of Wushu and dance and has clear features of the Central-China Plains. This is the best drama in which Wushu is played so well.

By Li Changchun
Member of the Standing Committee of Central Political Bureau

In *Shaolin in the Wind*, there are many creations in both its content and form. It is one of the most excellent dramas produced in recent years. This drama has combined polite letters and martial art, toughness and gentleness. It touches people with love, moves people with dance and shocks people with skill. It makes art enjoyable.

By Xu Guangchun
Secretary of the CPC's Henan Provincial Committee,
Chairman of the Standing Committee of Henan Provincial People's Congress

The Shaolin heroic spirit demonstrated by such a touching and grand scene is rare and is needed in present dramas. The exploration in uniting Wushu with dance is very valuable.

By Yu Ping
Director of Art Department of Ministry of Culture

This drama is elaborately designed, produced and performed, and it is touching and shocking.

By Jia Zuoguang
Honorary Chairman of China Dance Association

After I watched this dance drama, I felt that the creation of dance drama in China has entered a new era and *Shaolin in the Wind* is a milestone.

By Zhao Qing
Vice-chairman of China Dance Association

This drama is so well performed, so powerful, so profound beyond my expectation. Its innovation of combining Wushu with dance is significant and it is a beautiful flower among Chinese dance dramas.

By Xu Peidong
Secretary of China Music Association Party Division, Famous Composer

Comments on the Top Ten of "National Fine Stage Works of Art Project 2005-06":

Another feature of the fine works selected in this year is that all of them have explored and created bravely new elements and forms of art, carried forward the stage style and the performance skills with the time. The dance drama *Shaolin in the Wind* draws materials from a well-known Shaolin Kung Fu story, and combines dance and Wushu. It displays the perfect craft of synthesis by infusing love, Ch'an martial art, meditation and revenge into one.

All these fine works are also warmly welcomed by the audience and have bought favorable influence to the drama market greatly. The acrobatics drama *Swan Lake* and the dance drama *Shaolin in the Wind* have both achieved good social and economic profits. *Shaolin in the Wind* has been performed for 75 times both at home and abroad, and its proceeds have reached 11,270,000 RMB *yuan*.

小记

这本书也算应命之文，草记关于这座城市历史、艺术的杂感，也多少记录了《风中少林》的足迹。成文中阮志斌先生做了大量的文字工作，文中"相关链接"部分常松木先生提供了大量资料，也参考了相关书籍和网站，在此一并表示谢意。

图书在版编目（CIP）数据

风中舞动少林/齐岸青著. —郑州：大象出版社，
2007.7
ISBN 978 – 7 – 5347 – 4778 – 6

Ⅰ.风…　Ⅱ.齐…　Ⅲ.散文—作品集—中国—当代
Ⅳ.I267

中国版本图书馆 CIP 数据核字（2007）第 099496 号

责任编辑　吴韶明
责任校对　李建平　方　丽
装帧设计　刘 & 王
出版发行　大象出版社（郑州市经七路 25 号　邮政编码 450002）
网　　址　www.daxiang.cn
制　　版　郑州普瑞印刷制版服务有限公司
印　　刷　河南省瑞光印务股份有限公司
版　　次　2007 年 7 月第 1 版　2007 年 7 月第 1 次印刷
开　　本　787 × 1092　1/16
印　　张　11.5
印　　数　1—3 200 册
定　　价　120.00 元
若发现印、装质量问题，影响阅读，请与承印厂联系调换。
印厂地址　郑州市二环支路 35 号
邮政编码　450012　　　　电话　(0371)63955319